D0101459

KNIGHTMARES

by

Rich Wolfe

www.ohwhataknight.com

Contents

Contents

Preface

Sports in America, in general, have run amok. Just a few years ago, Barry Alvarez led the University of Wisconsin's football team to victory in the Rose Bowl and was voted the National Coach of the Year. Meanwhile in Columbus, Ohio, the fans were ready to run Ohio State Coach John Cooper out of town—again. Ohio State and Wisconsin had exactly the same record that year: 10–1–1. One guy was the National Coach of the year; the other guy—the fans wanted to tar and feather. In the United States, there are far more sports writers than religious reporters. Put that in the "Go Figure" file . . . under the category "Basketball is Almost a Religion in Indiana."

This is my sixth book in the last four years. In none of the previous books has there ever been anything really negative about any of the subjects. However, when it comes to Bob Knight, a book would have no credibility if it did not deal with the controversial aspects of his career.

Thus, the conundrum was, "How do you do a fair book on Bob Knight and cover all his scrapes with the players, administrators, fellow coaches, and even the law?" It also became evident early on that a book on Bob Knight would be aimed mainly at the people who reside outside the state of Indiana. In the summer of 2000, the Hatfields and McCoys were transformed into Knight and anti-Knight camps in the Hoosier state giving new meaning to Indiana's state slogan: The Crossroads of America.

I had never seen such a controversy since the O. J. Simpson murder trial. Who can forget that? I remember the day back in the summer of 1994 when a friend said a famous ex-football player had murdered his wife. (Immediately, I prayed that it was Frank Gifford.) Shortly after that trial got underway, and long before a verdict was reached, a very interesting book was written by Sheila Weller, called *Raging Heart*. In this book she examined controversial episodes of O. J. and Nicole Simpson's life together and merely quoted both sides as their friends saw it. She drew no conclusions whatsoever.

Thus while comparing the controversy and divisiveness of the Simpson trial to the Bob Knight ongoing and simmering debate in Indiana the past summer, the thought came: Why not do the Knight book the same way? Just talk to the friends and enemies, and let the chips fall where they may.

I have no reason to believe that any of the people in Knightmares lied. With the exception of one person, most of them were calm as they discussed their problems with Coach Knight. I'm certainly not here to vouch for them. It's just that I have no reason to disbelieve them.

In an effort to get more material into the book, the editor decided to merge certain paragraphs and omit some commas which will allow for the reader to receive an additional 30,000 words, the equivalent of 80 pages. More bang for your buck, more fodder for English teachers, less dead trees.

When all is said and done, remember this is just a book. It's a book to entertain you. It's not a treatise. It's not a bible. It's not a declaration of absolute facts. It's just Bob Knight as seen through the eyes of other people. I have no dog in this hunt. So don't get any ideas about shooting the messenger. On the other hand, if you have some good constructive criticism, feel free to jot it on the back of a twenty-dollar bill and send it along to the publisher.

Go now.

Rich Wolfe
Scottsdale, Arizona

Bibliography

Albom, Mitch. *The Fab Five:* Warner Books, 1993
Alford, Steve and John Garrity. *Playing for Knight:* Simon and Shuster, 1989.
Feinstein, John. *A Season on the Brink:* Macmillan, 1986.
Hammel, Bob. *Beyond the Brink:* Indiana University Press, 1987.
Jamison, Steve. *Wooden:* Contemporary Press, 1997.
Keteyian, Armen and Alexander Wolff. *Raw Recruits:* Pocket Books, 1990.
Meyer, Ray and Ray Sons. *Coach:* Contemorary, 1987.
Mylenski, Skip. *Winning at Illinois:* Sagamore, 1987.
Odom, David. *The End is Not the Trophy:* Carolina Academic Press, 1998.
Pluto, Terry. *Tark:* McGraw-Hill, 1988.
Scanion, Pat. *Digger Phelps and Notre Dame Basketball:* Prentice-Hall, 1981.
Wartenberg, Steve. *Winning is an Attitude:* St. Martins, 1991.
Weiss, Dick. *Campus Chaos:* Time Out Press, 2000.
Weiss, Dick. *Full Court Pressure:* Hyperion, 1992.
Weiss, Dick. *Refuse to Lose:* Ballantine, 1996.

The author would like to sincerely thank the following authors, subjects and/or publishers for their kind permission to cite, reprint or quote from their works:

Carter, Cris and Butch. *Born to Believe:* Full Wits Publishing, Inc., Upper Tantallon, Nova Scotia.
Douchant, Michael. *Tourney Time:* Masters Press, 1993.
Feinstein, John. *A March to Madness:* Little Brown & Co., 1998.
Gildea, William. *Where the Matters Most:* Little Brown & Co., 1997.
Golenbock, Peter. *Personal Fouls:* Carroll & Graf, 1990.
Guest, Larry. *Confessions of a Coach:* Rutledge Hill, 1991.
Johnson, Roy S. *Outrageous:* Simon & Shuster, 1992.
Kirkpatrick, Curry. *Just Your Average, Bald, One-Eyed, Basketball Wacko:* Simon & Shuster, 1998.
Monteith, Mark. *Passion Play:* Bonus Books, 1988.
Mortimer, Jeff. *Basket Case:* Doubleday, 1988.
Phelps, Teresa Godwin. *Coach's Wife:* W.W. Norton, 1994.
Ryan, Bob. *Drive:* Doubleday, 1989.
Savage, Jim. *The Encyclopedia of the NCAA Basketball Tournament:* Dell, 1990.
Sperber, Murray. *The Chronicle of Higher Education:* May, 2000.
Weiss, Dick. *Holding Court:* Masters Press, 1995.
Weiss, Dick. *Time Out:* Berkley Books, 1992.
Wojciechowski, Gene. *Pond Scum and Vutures:* Macmillan, 1990.
Yaeger, Don. *Tiger in a Lion's Den:* Hyperion, 1994.

These Guys Are Declarin' Shenanigans

Russ Brown
Gene Wojciechowski
John Feinstein
Terry Reed
Murray Sperber
Pat Williams
Clair Recker

Calling Bob Knight "Bobby" is like calling Attila the Hun "Tilly"

Russ Brown

Russ Brown of the Louisville Sports Report *was born, raised and still resides in Indiana. He covered Indiana basektball for 14 years for* The Louisville Courier Journal *and makes no secret of his disdain for Coach Knight.*

Russ Brown

I can remember the very first time I ever talked with Knight in my life and it went downhill from there. He got the job at Indiana and a friend of mine, a mutual friend who is now dead, John Flynn, knew Knight when he was assistant high school coach in Ohio. John had the best line about Knight I've heard so far. He wrote a story for the Courier-Journal Sunday Magazine, which is no longer published, and in it he said, "Calling Bob Knight 'Bobby' is like calling Attila the Hun 'Tilly'."

Some do call him Bobby; I never called him that—always Bob. Flynn was a Knight defender and, I think, liked him—realized what he was, yet liked him. It was kinda funny, because for all my bad relations with Knight, we had two really good mutual friends. I used to always debate with them—Billy Reed, a sportswriter for Sports Illustrated in Lexington, was a good friend and also a friend of Knight's. And John was a friend of Knight's and, also, a real good friend of mine. We didn't see eye-to-eye on Knight at all.

When Knight was hired at IU, John Flynn and I both worked at the Louisville Courier-Journal. John said, "I'll get Bob on the phone for you." This was the day after he got the job—that night. So John got him on the phone, and I got on. Of course, he didn't any more want to talk to me than the man in the moon, but I got on and asked him a legitimate question. George McGinnis, IU's sensational sophomore, was thinking about going pro and there was a lot of talk that spring that he would go pro. I had probably asked Knight a couple of innocuous questions. I can't remember how I phrased the question. But I asked Knight what were his thoughts about the possibility that George McGinnis would go pro. He said, "That's a dumb

10

fuckin' question." And it went downhill from there. It was the first time any source had talked to me like that. I thought maybe this guy was—John had told me that he was volatile. I hadn't heard all that much about him, and I just couldn't believe the guy had done that. What's the point here? Why would you talk to somebody like that? Why wouldn't you just say, "I can't answer that." Or something like that. I tell people all the time, "I never have in my life, either personal or professional life, dealt with anybody who even remotely approached Knight for mean-spiritedness, for purposely putting people in uncomfortable positions, relishing confrontation. Most people avoid confrontation; he seeks it out."

That's been so long ago—1971. I think when I got off the phone and said something to John, he just laughed. You have to know John, but he just laughed about it. But it really wasn't a laughing matter to me. I just couldn't believe the guy would talk that way to somebody he had never met. That was not a stupid question. It was a legitimate question that you would ask the coach who was taking over any program. I don't know this for sure, but I'm sure he got asked about it when he finally did a formal press conference.

I can't remember the first time I met Knight, which is kinda strange. I can say I didn't like him. John and I had these conversations all the time. Knight is a very difficult person to like. Unless he's turned on the charm with recruiting, and I've seen him when he is trying to be charming, he's very hard to like. I supposed the first time I ever saw him personally was during his first formal press conference at IU and I don't remember anything about it except here was this guy that I thought was very sullen, very boorish, sarcastic, smart ass—even during his first press conference. That's the way I came away.

I tell people that nobody is all good and all bad—I'm willing to admit that. I just have a hard time, because I've been around him so much, and seen how he has treated people and seen how he manipulates—that alleged apology and the whole latest situation at the University is just typical of him. I can't find a lot of good to say about him. In defending him, people say, "Oh, but he does a lot of good for people and blah, blah, blah." Well, Maybe. But so what!

To me, you judge people on how they treat people on a daily basis and not just by a few good deeds they do here and there that he probably thinks cancels out the bad stuff. It's like people who go to church on Sunday, and feel like that absolves them of all the sins of the first six days. You'll never hear anything sincere come out of Knight's mouth—any kind of an apology. He's already started now; he's already mounted his offensive now against this new ruling by the University. He said he was not going to teach that class in

basketball anymore because he's under this "zero tolerance". I haven't figured out what that has to do with it. I guarantee you—mark my word—he
will not have press conferences this year. He will not have post-game press
conferences. I'll bet you he won't. That will be one of his ways of "I'll show
you!"

You couldn't be a "beat" writer and do your job and have any kind of
relationship with him because he wouldn't allow it. He sees things in black
and white, you're either for him or against him. If you're for him, you'll cover
up anything or not write certain things. If you're against him, you couldn't be
objective in his eyes. Again it would be either for or against him.

I covered him from his very first year until after they lost to Virginia in
the NCAA so about fourteen LONG years! He would call the house, and it
would be funny if it weren't so. . . . My wife would answer and he'd be real
nice, "Oh, Hi Mrs. Brown, how are you? Could I speak to Russ?" Then I'd
get on the phone. "You little son of a bitch! You fucker! Don't you ever come
up here anymore! I'll ram your fuckin' head through the locker room wall."
Oh, he threatened me on a number of occasions.

The Courier-Journal was always there for me. Did I want to sue him for
wanton endangerment? No, I didn't want to do that. Now if he had ever laid
a hand on me, I would have.

It was an Illinois game, probably '77–'78; Illinois had a good team that
year, and it was a good game, and Indiana won. *60 Minutes* was there doing
a profile of him. Dan Rather was on the program at that time. Knight was
kinda flying high—they had won. So he walks into the interview room, and
this was on *60 Minutes;* I always sit in the front row—always ask the first
question. I wasn't about to let him intimidate me. So Knight came up to me
and said, "I really feel good. I feel so good, Russ, that I'm even gonna shake
your hand and ask you how your family is and how you're doing." I said, "Well
you must feel pretty damn good then." So that was the end of that part of it.
I think that part was on *60 Minutes*. He did that because it was a "show" plus
he had won a pretty big game. So he gets up and he does his press conference. He goes out and stands outside the interview room.

Lou Henson, the Illinois Coach, comes in and I listen a little to Henson,
then I get up to go to the locker room. I walk past Knight; he doesn't say a
word. I get maybe fifteen yards down the hall, maybe; this is in Assembly
Hall, and he says, "Hey Russ." So I turn around and he's got this pistol
pointed at me, and he fires it. There is concrete on both walls and the sound
is—just whap, whap, whap, whap—just reverberates—loud as hell. I said,
"You missed." He said, "Wait till you shake your head." I had a job to do so I

just turned around and kept going to the locker room. I know this sounds weird, and people always say, "Weren't you scared?" This is why I don't think it was done maliciously. He didn't give me time to really think "Uh-oh, that son of a bitch is going to kill me." It was like, I turned around, as I recall, and almost immediately he fired. Bob Pille from the Chicago Sun Times was standing next to Knight, and said, "Bob, you're crazy." Knight said, "I've got to be crazy to keep from going insane." I think that's an old Willie Nelson line or something. It's funny, because he's never mentioned it to me; I've never mentioned it to him. I think it was his way of apologizing or sort trying to mend fences or whatever and that was just sort of his way—his sense of humor.

As I recall, it wasn't like he pointed at me—like I've got you now—I'm gonna kill you or whatever. He's crazy enough that I probably would have thought—course he would have gotten off Scot-free. I mean, he kills a reporter—BIG DEAL! I mean, at Bloomington, he's winning—didn't matter. Shooting a reporter— he *might* get charged; he'd probably get off.

There was another time—this is kinda funny, too. I had written some stories that he didn't like and he called me and said, "If I ever see you around here, I'm gonna run your fuckin' head through the locker room wall. I don't ever want to see you again. And blah, blah, blah." So the next game was away—Notre Dame at South Bend. I can't remember who won. I was there in my usual spot—front row at the press conference. Well he comes in and says, "Has anybody got a question?" I asked the first question, Knight doesn't even look at me—says, "Does anybody else have a question?" So I ask the question again. And again, "Does anybody else have a question?" I said, "Does that mean you're not going to answer my question? He said, "That's right." At that point then, you either back down or 'cause a scene so I didn't say anything else.

So that was sort of our relationship.

He doesn't talk to anybody really. I mean he doesn't give you access. I've been in this business thirty five years. Covering the Indiana basketball team is the worst job in America. You have no access. You've got to put up with his bullshit all the time. If he would at least talk about or discuss with people some of the things he does, or answer questions about them, it would at least make the job maybe a little more bearable.

For instance, the time he went to Illinois and benched all his starters. I think Alford was one of them. Then afterward he never would talk about it. He wouldn't answer questions. He didn't come to the press conference. That's so typical.

Then there's the Puerto Rican incident. I wasn't there, but I will guarantee you that it happened just like the policeman said it happened. He tried to pull his power play on the guy, and the guy wouldn't have any of it. You know, Knight wants to say that he was the victim. Bull. Anybody that knows him and knows how he. . . . I mean you can just see how that all played out. He comes in. The women are still in there practicing. He throws one of his childish temper tantrums and they arrest him.

John Flynn told me this story: He had talked to the grandmother who virtually raised Knight. He said the grandmother told him that anytime they played a game when Knight was a child, the grandmother would let him win because if he didn't win, he'd throw a temper tantrum and throw the board, and destroy the game and all that. My theory in part is—I think the guy's got a screw loose—but on top of that, he found out at a very early age that if he talked dirtier and yelled louder than anybody else he could pretty much get his own way.

Lou Henson called him a "classic bully." And that's basically what he is. He's found out that if he employed all those tactics he used as a child in adulthood, it would get him what he wanted. On top of that, he did win early. Indiana is just a "rabid" basketball state, a lot of people who don't see beyond the wins. We, the writers who cover him, have always said "As long as he is winning, we were joking during his prime, he could have shot a player on the basketball floor. And fans would have said "That's okay, the player deserved it, he traveled or whatever." "Coach was right." It's just that simple-minded attitude and the University has gotten themselves into a position where there's either nobody willing or considered powerful enough to stand up to him— from Presidents on down. And he just found out he could do virtually anything he wanted. And did, and then would make excuses for his behavior, and his followers AND the University would make excuses for it.

Looking at the whole list of what he has done, can you imagine any other University in the country tolerating that? Or can you imagine anybody holding a job who behaved like that?

How could you walk in and throw something at a secretary and keep your job? And talk to people the way he talks to them—the foul language and everything—you couldn't; there's no way. He's got the only job in America he could keep and act the way he does.

Early on when I would go back to Louisville and explain what was going on, my bosses believed me. The publisher at the time, Barry Bingham, wrote a letter to Knight one time about his threats toward me. Bingham got back this bizarre letter—just a childish and bizarre letter—that Knight had signed it "Mickey Mouse," with copies to Donald Duck, Pluto—just some weird stuff. This is just an example.

Here's another story. My sister, a student at Purdue at the time, was 32 or 33 and was killed in an auto accident. My mother and dad were on an airplane; they live in Indianapolis. Knight got on the plane, and he was talking to people and came to our parents. They told him they were my parents, "We're Russ Brown's parents." He said, "Oh, I'm so sorry to hear about your daughter." I saw him several days later—walked into the rest room; we were peeing in adjoining urinals and he not only did not say a word to me about "sorry to hear about your sister" or "I gave your Mom and Dad my condolences", he jumped on me about something I had written, "How can you write such stupid fuckin' stuff?" It's mind-boggling. Why would the guy be nice enough to my parents to say something like that? Then see me, and know that I'd just lost a sister, and treat me like that. He's so mean spirited.

I got to the point where I hated going up to Bloomington. I grew up in Indiana; I've been an IU basketball fan all my life. But I just got to the point where I just despised doing it. I finally went to my sports editor and said, or I think they even asked me, "Would you consider another assignment?" But people always thought that I got off the Indiana beat because of my conflicts with Knight and that was not the case. The real reason I wanted off was I could no longer stand being around the guy and seeing how he treated people. I'm a big boy. I can deal with whatever he can dish out, even though it made my job miserable. But just seeing how he treated people on a day to day basis and being around his arrogance and his bulliness and his mean-spiritedness—I just didn't want to do it anymore. Why do I need this? I don't need to be around somebody like this.

I don't know his current wife. It was kinda funny, because even during the periods when Knight wouldn't talk to me or when he was calling me and threatening me, his first wife was always real nice to me. She would come down to the press box and talk to me, and I wanted to say to her, "Nancy, do you realize your husband won't have anything to do with me?" She would tell me that she would hide newspapers from him so he wouldn't see some stories and get upset.

Nancy still lives in Bloomington, as far as I know. I don't think she ever remarried. Bill Benner, of the Indianapolis Star, and I have always thought—if anybody could ever talk her into writing a book—you talk about a best seller! My God. It would be. . . . But I don't think she'd ever do it.

She was not an unattractive lady, not beautiful, but I always liked her. I felt she was a little bit crazy, too, but she'd have to be after living with him. I never heard any stories about him screwing around; I will say that. I never got the impression from him or friends or anybody that he even talked about women. I think he, basically, hates women.

One time he took a dump in the middle of the floor (this came from a player) and said to his players, "You guys are playing like shit and now you're gonna have to play in it." Those were his words. I know it's accurate—real accurate, came from a player.

Then there's the tampon story with Landon Turner. He put a tampon in Landon Turner's locker because he had told him he was playing like a pussy. There's probably more to it than that. A lot of people would be tickled to death if he got his comeuppance, so to speak. I think there are a lot of people who dislike him, who don't respect him and a lot of other things but are too nice, too intimidated or whatever to say anything derogatory about him.

Even when I was covering him, I was honest about him if somebody asked me. I probably wasn't as outspoken as I am now, but I wasn't gonna sit there and tell people he's a nice guy. And people knew, it was common knowledge, that we didn't get along. Of course, he didn't get along with anybody that tried to do a good job. After the gun incident, I think he was civil to me for a while, but his idea of being civil and anybody else's are two different things really.

This is interesting—a friend of mine has told me that Knight's secretary (this is all second-hand information) told a mutual friend that Knight was more uptight and angry than ever this summer of 2000, and "he'll never make it." Knight is so jealous of Alford. He can't stand the fact that Alford is so well liked in this state, so personable. And the fact that when Alford was coming into Assembly Hall and overshadowing Knight. The way he treated Steve Alford was just typical—that's about all you can say about that.

You know why Luke Recker did what he did in waiting 'til Knight was out of the country before faxing his transfer? He tried to quit after his freshman year, and Knight told him—now this is just childish, and I can't believe Recker would fall for it—"If you quit, I'm gonna resign, and I'm gonna tell everybody that you're the reason I'm resigning and your name will be mud in this state." So Luke starts feeling guilty about it, doesn't quit and then the next year when he wants to quit, waits 'til Knight's out of the country and faxed his transfer. That's why Recker did it then.

Luke Recker was almost killed in an automobile accident. His girlfriend is paralyzed; her brother's in a coma. Knight has never ever once called Recker, called Recker's family, offered any kind of sympathy or anything. Wouldn't play in the golf tournament that Recker had to benefit them.

These things I'm telling you are not from rumors; they came from really good sources. I also have it from a good source, and anybody with brains could figure it out. The only reason Indiana didn't finally stand up and say to him, "You're fired." The attorneys, in fact I was told Knight didn't go to the President's home to apologize at all; he went to threaten a lawsuit. Because the whole deal was, not in these words, "you've let me get by with this kind of behavior, you've tacitly approved it. If you fire me, I'm gonna file a two hundred and fifty million dollar lawsuit against you," or whatever it was.

I don't know what will happen with Coach Felling—I would guess they'll pay him to go away or settle out of court, I think that's what they'll do.

One time Knight didn't like something Kit Klingelhoffer, the IU Sports Information Director, had put on a quote sheet or in a release, came storming into Kit's office, started berating him and screaming at him, knocked him down and out cold. Then the next day, Kit comes in, and there's about half a dozen new dress shirts on his desk from Knight. That's the way he is.

Clarence Doninger, the current Athletic Director, was his personal attorney; he's the one who helped him out of the Puerto Rican mess and with his divorce. Now they don't even talk. Not all these people could be wrong. Give me a break. Then with the Neil Reed situation—he would have gotten off on that. They were all ready to sweep that under the rug, but then Felling had the tape. Felling had saved the tape and gave it to ESPN or CNN or whoever it was. If not for that tape, Knight would be walking Scot-free on that. This type thing happened over and over with other kids. These kids come in, they leave. All of a sudden, the machinery kicks into full gear. All of a sudden the kid's a bad kid, or he's a troublemaker, or he couldn't play—one thing after another—character assassination is what it is. Too bad that some of the players who have credibility won't speak out. Most of the guys who speak out are guys who have left for one reason or another. I know for a fact _____ can't stand him but would _____ ever say anything bad about him—no.

There's something mentally wrong with Knight. People don't act like that who are sane and have any sense. I don't think anything could have happened to him to mess him up as badly as he's messed up.

You know I just never—I'm 55 years old—I've never felt about anybody the way I feel about that guy. I think he's an evil person—I really do. I wouldn't put anything past him if he thought it was going to further his agenda, or make him look better, or feed his ego, or whatever. I'll admit it.

I don't have a whole lot good to say about the guy. Hammel wrote that pseudo-apology back in May after the first flap—Knight didn't write that. Hammel wrote it. If you ever get hold of Hammel, ask him point blank; make him lie to you, 'cause Knight didn't write it. It was the "apology that wasn't an apology." How could any reasonable person read this and think that it's a sincere apology?

Mike Ditka had to apologize last year. He grabbed his crotch or something. But it wasn't written or anything else. You knew that he meant it—knew he was sincere about it.

Knight won't see anything in your book that is negative as the truth. I don't think he'll read it in the first place, but people will tell him about it.

In my opinion, his arrogance, and ego and pride are keeping him from mending his fences with Steve Alford, Krzyzewski and others. If they came to him, and begged his "forgiveness" and got down on their knees to the great "God of Basketball" then maybe he would do it. But he's not gonna do it.

Take the way he insulted John Wooden. John Wooden is one of the best, most kind, most anything you can say good about a person. During that interview last May, Roy Firestone asked him what he thought about John Wooden saying he didn't approve of Knight's message and wouldn't let a son of his play for him or words to that effect. And Knight said, "If Pete Newell said that, I'd be concerned about it, but Wooden's never been to one of my practices, never seen many of my games, etc." Well, here's a guy who's a fine human being, a fine example for everybody and has won more championships than Knight can ever hope to—and that's part of the problem right there. He knows he can never equate with Wooden and for him to make some asinine. . . . I read a column that referred to it as a "jaw-dropping insult" to John Wooden, and that's basically what it was.

There was a short-lived Conference Commissioner's Association tournament and Indiana played in it one year in St. Louis. They played Southern California when USC was coached by Bob Boyd. Knight gets up at the press conference. Course this is typical, too. He always praises coaches he can beat. You never heard him praise anybody that beat his ass. Well, Bill Frieder did that. He told me one time that he got along fine with Knight—until Frieder's team started beating his. By that time Wooden had already five or six or maybe even seven NCAA titles. Knight gets up at the press conference and talked about the game, and—this is true—he called Bob Boyd the best damn basketball coach on the West Coast. Now Bob "Fuckin'" Boyd! Who is that? He's some crony of Knight's that Knight knows he can beat; he's insanely jealous of John Wooden so he gets up and insults Wooden. I couldn't believe it. Then he makes those remarks about Wooden—Pete Newell—who's Pete Newell?—Yeah, he's a good basketball coach but nothing compared to John Wooden. It's just typical. Back in the days when John Powell was at Wisconsin, Harv Schmidt was at Illinois and some of those stiffs who couldn't coach anything, and he would get up after he had beaten them by 40 or 50 points and talk about what great coaches they were and how people in Madison, Wisconsin or Champaign, Illinois or wherever ought to get off their ass. (Insinuating they were so good!) Well, yeah, he was beating the shit out of them. You won't ever hear him defending Gene Keady or Steve Fisher or Bill Frieder or Lou Henson or any of the people who could beat him with some regularity.

One of the untold stories about the Fred Taylor (Knight's college coach at Ohio State) situation was Knight could not stand—and this came via John Flynn directly from Knight—Fred Taylor. These days you would think Taylor was Knight's best friend, until Taylor died recently. Knight couldn't stand him until another coach Knight respected told Knight before he ever got to Army, "If you ever want to get anywhere in the coaching business, you better make peace with Fred Taylor." So that's how that all came about.

I know a former associate athletic director at Army, who lives in Louisville now, and I was talking to him just last year. After the Neil Reed reprimand deal, I said. "You know J. C."—a retired general or something—"a lot of people say that Knight just brought that military mentality to Indiana, and he could get by with anything. That all kind of sprouted at Army." But my friend said Knight was in trouble at Army; he had been called in and told "any more incidents and you're history" because of some of the things that he had pulled at West Point. So it started long before he came to Indiana.

To let somebody treat people like that, what kind of a person are you? What kind of a school or anything else? It's stuff you can't get by with in real life. You couldn't do any of what Knight did if you worked for a company or a corporation and get by with it. The first thing they'll tell you is "he runs an honest program and he graduates the players." Well that shouldn't be an excuse or justification, it should be expected.

(Brown was re-interviewed after the firing.)

I think it should have happened a long, long time ago. I can't believe that they let it go on as long as they did. I watched the ESPN thing, and I can sum it up in about two or three sentences. According to Knight, everybody else lies. It's everybody else's fault. He took no responsibility. No accountability. I don't know; it's just weird. He and some of his friends want to portray him as this innocent victim who was targeted by this bad administration. When he grabbed the kid, I told *everybody* that they had two choices. They either gotta ignore it, or they gotta fire him. Because if they admit it happened with the kid, obviously it violates zero tolerance. Now they could have done what they've done with him so many times—ignore it. But they only had these two choices. They had to ignore it or fire him. They couldn't admit that it happened and then say, "Well, we're gonna give him another chance."

I think a lot of people, even IU fans, are glad they finally got rid of him. He was losing a lot of support. In the last few years, in fact, I rarely, and this is a real change, talked to an Indiana fan who didn't want him out of there. They said, "We're tired of his bull shit, and he's not winning." Not winning was probably the bottom line. I think IU would be better off getting rid of him.

I think, and I haven't really polled anybody, if you're not an Indiana fan, you got to feel like it's a good thing. He doesn't have a lot of followers outside of the Hoosier faithful. I think he is evil and extremely mean spirited and yeah, evil's a good way to describe him—very evil. He's still got his defenders, and I still don't know how anybody could justify or rationalize that kind of behavior. I was glad to see it happen. I guarantee you though that somebody will hire him.

The Write Stuff

Gene Wojciechowski

Gene Wojciechowski is currently the top basketball writer for ESPN the Magazine. Prior to that he was a Sports Illustrated writer.

L et me begin by saying that Bobby Knight is one of the finest coaches ever to wear an ill-fitting sweater that emphasizes a prodigious beer gut—bar none. And while I've never chosen an Indiana University team to win our office NCAA basketball pool, I can admit a certain fondness for the Hoosiers' man-to-man defense and Knight's insistence on running a pristine program.

As for the numbskull things Knight has had to say about sportswriters, well . . .

Fact is fact: With the exception of Puerto Rican police officers, I can think of nobody whom Knight despises more than someone carrying a press pass and an independent thought.

It was Knight who once said of sports reporters: "All of us learn to write in the second grade. Most of us then go on to greater things."

Like basketball, which we learned to play in third-grade gym class?

And it is Knight who mostly treats sportswriters as if they were dirty jockstraps. To Knight's way of thinking, you are either for him or against him. And if you choose the latter, God help you.

Is Knight a great coach? Undoubtedly, A humanitarian? Often. A writer's best friends? Are you kidding?

If I had a son who wanted to play college basketball, I'd want him to play for Knight. However, if he wanted to be a sportswriter *and* cover Knight's Indiana team, I'd tell him to consider the wonderful world of aluminum siding.

This is the problem with covering college hoops: The coaches become the stars, not the players. Players come and go. Coaches stay, as do their sometimes-dictatorial ways when dealing with the Fourth Estate. Knight is merely president of the club.

Knight's most publicized tirades involved sportswriter John Feinstein, who wrote *A Season on the Brink.* Knight hated the book and hated Feinstein for writing it. At one point Knight accused Feinstein of being a pimp. Later, Knight accused him of being a whore.

"Well," said Feinstein, "I wish he'd make up his mind so I'd know how to dress."

It wasn't always that way. There was a time when Knight and Feinstein almost were pals.

Back before the book was published, Knight and Feinstein were leaving the University of Illinois basketball arena after an important Hoosiers victory when they were stopped by autograph seekers. Under normal circumstances, Knight might have signed a few scraps of paper and moved on.

But this was different. His Indiana team had won a big game and by doing so had beaten Illinois coach Lou Henson, whom Knight disliked—a lot. Knight was in a buoyant mood and happily signed away. As he did one of the autograph workers turned to Feinstein and said, 'Hey, Coach, can we get you, too?"

Feinstein, who obviously had been mistaken for an IU assistant, shook his head no.

With that, the autograph seeker turned to a friend and said, "Get this, Knight signs, but this asshole won't."

Knight roared with laughter when he heard that one. As it turns out, it would be about the last time he cracked a smile at anything involving Feinstein.

Knight was always picking on somebody. If it wasn't Feinstein, it was Russ Brown. If it wasn't Brown, it was *Sports Illustrated's* Curry Kirkpatrick.

Kirkpatrick made the mistake (at least, in Knight's eyes) of appearing on *60 Minutes* and offering a less favorable view of the fabled Knight. And although the program hadn't been aired when Kirkpatrick attended an IU game on the final day of the season, Knight acted hostile, as if he had been told the content of Kirkpatrick's taped interview with Rather.

This was the year (1980) that IU won the Big Ten championship on the final day of the regular season. Kirkpatrick was on deadline, but decided to attend Knight's post game press conference and then return to his typewriter at courtside. Bad move.

Kirkpatrick had just settled into his seat when Knight stomped into the room. The coach began to discuss the game and Kirkpatrick, head down, began scribbling notes. A few moments later he heard, "Kirkpatrick, what are you doing here?"

Kirkpatrick looked up and smiled. How nice of Knight to notice him, he thought.

Problem was, Knight wasn't smiling back. In fact, Knight began a profanity-laden speech that was directed entirely at Kirkpatrick.

Knight wanted the writer out of the room. He even threatened to end the press conference if Kirkpatrick didn't leave immediately.

"I want you all to know that I'm not saying one more word until that asshole leaves and you all know who I mean."

Kirkpatrick gathered his things. "In deference to my colleagues, I'll leave." He said. "I'm leaving, but I'm leaving for those people's sake, not yours."

"You're leaving because I told you so, asshole," Knight said.

Kirkpatrick made his way to courtside and started typing his story on a machine borrowed from another *Sports Illustrated* writer. The computer happened to have an SI logo on it. As he typed, several Indiana fans noticed the magazine logo and began heckling Kirkpatrick and throwing debris at him.

"Hey, SI, what do you think of that?" one of them yelled.

Another IU fan walked by and began slapping Kirkpatrick with a Hoosiers pennant. Tough day at work.

Sports Illustrated wrote a letter of protest to the Indiana University president, but that was about it. Kirkpatrick didn't mention the incident with Knight or the fans in his game story, which explains why Knight hugged him a few weeks later at the Final Four in Philadelphia. Knight, Kirkpatrick was told, apparently respected the writer's restraint enough so that he later sent Kirkpatrick an autographed copy of a book entitled, *All I Know About Coaching Basketball*.

The pages were blank.

All was well between Kirkpatrick and Knight until the 1984 Olympic Trials. That's when Knight, coach of the United States team, turned the try-out camp into a security stronghold. Guards, wearing suits and packing guns, patrolled the areas during practice. These were not pleasant people.

Somehow, Kirkpatrick lost his media credentials, but still managed to attend one of the workouts. As he stood talking with the other basketball writers, two of the armed guards approached him.

"Can we see your credentials?" asked one of the guards.

"Well, you see . . ."

The guards grabbed Kirkpatrick and tugged him away. They took him to a small room near the courts and kept him there.

"Who the hell are you guys?" said Kirkpatrick.

No response. At last one of them made a phone call, nodded, and led Kirkpatrick out onto the courts and to a tower occupied by, you guessed it, Knight, who used the vantage point to observe workout.

Basketballs stopped bouncing. Drills ceased. Knight looked down at Kirkpatrick and then tossed him the missing credentials.

"Fucking Kirkpatrick," he said, "you're just lucky I'm a nice guy."

The writers of *Sports Illustrated* always have had mixed success with Knight. Depending on the day and the most recent story about him or his IU program, Knight could be steamed or gracious. You never knew for sure until the moment he looked into your eyes or opened his mouth. Then the secret was out.

Jack McCallum once was sent to Bloomington by his SI editors to do a story on Hoosiers stars Ted Kitchel and Randy Wittman. Of course, any piece on any player at IU meant having to speak with Knight, which is easier said than done.

McCallum, who had never met Knight, began the process of arranging an interview with the famed coach. After about a dozen phone conversations with the school" sports information department, McCallum was told Knight would see him.

And then it hit McCallum: He would actually have to talk to Knight. The Bobby Knight. The great and all-powerful Knight. The Knight who had molded young men into whatever he wanted them to be, which takes one hell of a strong mold. That Knight.

The interview took place in the Indiana dressing room. McCallum asked his questions about Kitchel and Wittman, and much to the writer's surprise, Knight answered them. And politely, too.

McCallum let his mind wander ever so briefly. He wondered why he had ever been nervous about speaking with Knight in the first place. This guy was a pussycat, as soft as cashmere. Any more accommodating and he'd have to send Knight a thank-you note.

Knight started to describe each player on the Indiana roster. It was when he reached the name of Jim Thomas, a guard, that Knight's disposition took a turn for the worse.

"If I only could get Jim Thomas to . . ." said Knight, searching desperately for the right word, "To . . ."

Unable to adequately describe "killer instinct," Knight reached over and without warning grabbed McCallum's shirt and, with it, McCallum's necklace and a small handful of chest hairs. McCallum didn't know whether to cry or scream for help.

"You know, I want this from him!" said Knight.

"Hmmm," McCallum said, wincing.

It is hard to retain your dignity when valuable chest hairs are fluttering toward a locker room floor. But McCallum did his best. He had done nothing to offend Knight, yet the coach, in his own unmistakable way, had sent a message. Knight wanted McCallum to know that this was his domain, that McCallum was merely a guest and only marginally welcome, at that.

McCallum understood immediately.

For a number of reasons, the story on Kitchel and Wittman never ran. And for a number of reasons, including the amount of time Knight had given him, McCallum felt compelled to call to apologize.

"Bobby, you're not going to believe this," McCallum said, "but after all the time you gave me, the story isn't running."

McCallum expected a tempest. Instead he received a gentle breeze.

"I understand your business a lot better than you think I do," Knight said calmly. "I understand this happens all the time."

McCallum hung up the phone that day freshly intimidated and thoroughly confused. To this day, he understands Knight not one bit.

Knight is an Indiana treasure. They might as well designate his IU office a historical landmark, such is his appeal in Indiana and the surrounding region.

For example, when word leaked that Knight might accept an offer to coach at New Mexico, people went bonkers. They couldn't believe that their beloved Bobby would leave IU for anyplace else.

There were skeptics, including *Louisville Courier-Journal* columnist Rick Bozich, who thought that Knight was simply using the New Mexico offer to secure his standing at IU, to say nothing of having his ego enriched by concerned Hoosiers fans. So convinced was Bozich of Knight's intentions that he told a radio audience that very thing.

They take their basketball seriously in Indiana and Kentucky. Bozich had been threatened in anonymous letters and phone calls before, and there was little doubt that his comments about Knight might prompt similar action. And don't think his friends and neighbors didn't know it, either.

As Bozich pulled into his driveway after appearing on the radio show, he noticed a large cardboard sign attached to the utility pole that stood between his house and his neighbor. "Bozich lives here, "read the top of the sign, complete with an arrow that pointed toward the Bozich residence. "not here," read the bottom half, this time with an arrow pointed toward the neighbor" house.

You expect the unexpected when dealing with Knight. For instance, Rick Reilly of *Sports Illustrated* once was supposed to meet Knight for a 9:00 A.M. interview session. Knight was visiting Denver at the time, so Reilly arranged to be at the coach's hotel a little before nine.

The appointed hour came and went and Reilly, standing in the middle of the hotel lobby, began to worry. What if he had missed him? What if Bobby Knight, one of the country's most recognizable sports figures, had walked right past him? What would Reilly tell his editors?

At 9:45 Reilly raced to the house phones and called Knight's room. No answer. He hopped on an elevator and then knocked on Knight's door. There was the clicking of locks, soon followed by the grand sight of Knight in his birthday suit.

"C'mon in, I'm taking a shower," Knight said, "Talk to me now."

So Reilly, his glasses fogging with steam, sat on a toilet bowl and conducted an interview as America's most controversial coach lathered up.

Knight thought I was too snoopy; at least that's what he wrote in his diary

John Feinstein

In 1986, a young writer wrote a book that catapulted him and the Indiana basketball program to national prominence. The writer was John Feinstein, the book was A Season on the Brink. The result was a thoroughly irritated Coach Knight who surprisingly, as a result of the book, had more admirers than ever before.

Word circulated that Knight was upset that Feinstein had failed in his promise to seriously limit profanity and never thanked Knight for the incredible access granted.

The always erudite Feinstein was generous with his time as he addressed these accusations and other Knight problems.

You just have to understand Knight's psyche. I wasn't surprised that he was upset at me. Knight was just going to find something to be upset about because that's just the way he is. I was certainly surprised when he chose to make an issue out of his profanity because that's the least controversial thing about him. Everybody knows he uses profanity. That's just Bob; that's just the way he is. I was not surprised that he found something not to like; I was surprised by what he chose not to like.

My time in Bloomington was fascinating, very interesting because I was around people who are the best, or among the best, at what they do and I'm a basketball fan, and Knight's a great coach so it was an interesting experience. Fortunately I was single at the time so it wasn't as if I had to leave my family. Or move my family. It was just me. In Bloomington, I lived in a place called Dunnhill Apartments, right across from Assembly Hall. I've said often that I thought there were three coaches in the country who were interesting enough at the time to be worthy of a book like that: Knight, Dean Smith and John Thompson. I knew all three and knew of the three the only one who would even consider such a project was Knight. That's why I approached him.

Knight is one of these people who, he's a very black and white character, if he likes you, he likes you. If he doesn't, he doesn't. He liked me. I had a good relationship with him, and I think he honestly thought, correctly, that an inside look at his program would get the response that many people did ultimately have. It gave many people a more positive attitude about Knight. He's certainly got his flaws but he also has very positive things going for him.

On the other hand, no matter how many good things you do, it doesn't give you the right to break the law, to hit people, abuse people in any way. Bob seems to think it's okay, and one is not connected to the other. It's like the guy who owns the Washington Redskins. Dan Snyder got upset with me because I said he was a bully. He called me up and said you don't know how much charity work I do. I said, "so what does that have to do with anything?"

In regard to Knight supposedly being upset with profanity in the book: Number one, as I said a million times, when we discussed the issue of profanity, I said to him very specifically, "Bob, writing a book with you without the word 'fuck' would be like writing a book about you without the word 'bastard'." And he said, "Oh, I understand. I can go along with that." And I said, "no, because I want the book to be shorter than *War and Peace.*" And I left out eighty percent of his profanity and I never even used the word "cunt" which he uses all the time so in many ways. I did leave out a lot of profanity but I had to include some because otherwise people wouldn't take the book seriously. As far as the 'thank you note' was concerned, I never heard that one before to be honest. That's a bunch of crap. When the book first came out, I sent him a copy of it, before the book was published with a note saying "Here it is, hope you're happy with it. I think it accomplishes what you and I set out to do and obviously I couldn't have done it without the access you gave me." When I got the phone call, he didn't even call me himself, he had one of assistants call me, to say he was upset about the profanity, I wrote him another note saying "Look, Bob, if you're upset about something in this book, given everything you and I went through together, we should sit down and talk about it face to face, man to man. At the Notre Dame game that year, which was the first Indiana game I attended, Bob Hammel, who has been Bob's right-hand guy for years, came up and handed me an envelope. He said, "Bob wanted me to tell you that he refused to open your letter." As far as I was concerned that was the end of it.

Bob Knight is Bob Knight. I'm certainly not going to spend the rest of my life worrying about it—you move on. The only time I've made any attempt to contact him since then was when I wrote him a condolence note when his mother died. He did, six years ago in Hawaii, walk up and shake hands with me in a hotel and ask how I was doing and seemed to be very cordial. Since then whenever, I've seen him, we've exchanged hellos and kept going and that's been pretty much the end of it.

I don't know anybody who doesn't like Steve Alford. Bob can't stand for anybody's star to shine brighter than him. I got close to several players when I was there. I'm still good friends with Steve. I was pretty close to Daryl

Thomas and Todd Meier, certainly. Those were probably the three I knew best and I still keep in touch with Todd and Steve.

I was 28 when I did the book. This year I did another college basketball book called *The Least Known Division One Conference in America,* the Patriot Conference, which consisted of seven academic-oriented schools. I really got so tired of writing about 'pros in training,' I wanted to write about kids who really do go to college and play basketball and aren't gonna be pros and aren't gonna get rich off the sport and play the game because they love it. I had a very good time doing it.

When I was younger, I think I fantasized about someday writing books for a living, but I don't think I expected to have the success, especially right out of the box, based on the things I did. I know I worked hard, but I also have been very lucky. It's a matter of trying as a reporter to get to know how the people you are writing about think. I always try to be able when I finish a project I like to think I understand the people involved and know the subject involved as well as anybody. That's sort of my goal; I may not achieve it, but that's my goal. If I come close to achieving it and I can write like that, then I've done what I set out to do.

At the end of the book, when I left IU, I was on good terms with Bob Knight.

The NCAA changed the rules as a direct result of *A Season on the Brink.* The book described how Indiana kept practicing once they were eliminated from the NCAA Tournament . . . to get an early start for the next season. Technically, you could practice until the champion was crowned on the first Monday night in April. I think Knight was the only coach who understood that it was legal or might have been the only coach who saw the loophole. Once your season has ended these days you may not conduct practice. Before that, the rule simply said that no team could practice after the conclusion of the Final Four. They changed the rule because of Knight. Once your team has completed its season and played its last game you cannot hold formal practices. He felt it was legal; Knight would never break a rule.

In spite of plenty of evidence to the contrary, Bob still thinks he did absolutely nothing wrong. He is totally defiant, and he is not repentant. I don't see how you could expect anything different from Bob Knight. This is who he has been for 35 years as a head basketball coach. You know it was the chair's fault back in 1985. If you talk to Bob Knight about it and that's the whole problem. That's the crux of the problem There's never been anybody born who didn't do anything wrong. But because of the people around him, his friends/enablers who keep telling him that it's never his fault. Somebody else did something wrong. Someone's out to get him. In this case it's now Myles Brand. Bob honestly believes that he hasn't done anything wrong.

What do you think the chances are that Myles Brand wants to be remembered as the President of Indiana University who fired Bob Knight? If he builds the greatest library, the greatest history department in the history of higher education, he's gonna be remembered for one thing—He fired Bob Knight, and students burned him in effigy on the front lawn of his own home. He knew that something like that was gonna happen. That's why he didn't fire him in May. That's why he tried very hard to avoid firing him because he knew what was going to come down on him if he did. He tried everything he could, and, by the way, Myles Brand is as complicit in this as anybody because he never disciplined Bob Knight in any way before May nor did anybody else at Indiana. But he didn't want to fire Bob Knight because of what's happening right now.

Bob Knight never believed, nor did I, that it was really a zero tolerance policy; in fact it really wasn't. Because if it was zero tolerance, he would have been fired the minute he refused to deal with Clarence Doninger. He would have been fired the minute he raised his voice to that female lawyer. If you believe for a second, by the way, that he didn't raise his voice to her, then I've got some ocean-front land in Nebraska I'd really like to sell you. He believed that Indiana would let him continue to be Bob Knight and that every time something happened it would be someone else's fault. Frankly so did I!

For crying out loud, we're now into the semantics of what of what is zero tolerance. I'll tell you one thing zero tolerance is. It means you don't grab a kid you don't know. And now some of the Knight apologists are saying "well that was really no different than you know, patting a kid on the back during the course of a game." In another week, we're gonna find out that Knight was really inviting the kid into his office for tea and cookies.

If it was my kid, I'd be very upset. I'd be upset with my kid for addressing someone of that age and that rank disrespectfully, and I would tell him that. But I would also say, Wait a minute. If you want to turn around and say something in response, I don't have a problem with that. But the minute you put your hands on my kid, I have a serious problem with you, no matter who you are.

Bob's been taking cheap shots at people for years. The whole problem is this. Bob Knight is three things, without any debate: one of the greatest coaches ever, a guy who cares as much about academics as athletics in a time when that's very rare, and a guy who never broke an NCAA rule. But the fourth thing is: He's a self-righteous guy who thinks he can do no wrong and has a double standard for behavior. You behave one way toward me—respectfully, never be rude, always show me respect and loyalty, but I don't have to return any of that to you because I'm Bob Knight and you're not.

I think he could end up in a major program, and he absolutely will end up in a major program, if he takes the advice—and I thought Digger Phelps showed some guts by saying on television that he had advised Bob Knight to seek anger management counseling. Because if he had more friends do that before this occurred, he would still be the Indiana Coach. Because if his friends can get together and all those people out there he respects can convince him to do that, then there's no reason he can't get a major job. But even if he doesn't, he'll get a job, and it'll probably be a pretty good job because the president of a major university will stand up and will cite all that I have just cited that is positive and he'll say that Bob Knight has pledged that he will control his temper, and here's our new coach. And he'll sell lots of tickets and get lots of attention.

Even if he was being baited, under the terms of this alleged policy, he has to just walk away. The year I was with Knight, the one real bad blowup we had occurred on a Friday morning in Minneapolis when we were walking out of breakfast and a friend of Knight's had come to breakfast and he said to me, "So what are you going to do all day?" I said to him, "I'm going to do what I do every day; I'm going to follow Knight around." Knight was walking a couple of steps in front of us. I was not speaking to him, and I was not being disrespectful. He whirled on me, came back, put his finger in my face, and said, "Don't you ever address me that way. You can call me Coach, Coach Knight or Bob."

You see, this is the lunacy of him—lecturing anybody about manners. He doesn't have the credibility to lecture anybody about "manners and civility." His boorish behavior is well documented. He has no credentials on this.

If the run-in with the IU student is true, he didn't even get out of his own gym. It wasn't a question of what sportswriters would say; it wasn't a question of going on the road; it was on-campus, and he couldn't get out of his own gym. Time and time again, Bobby Knight said, "I can handle this. I know what this is about, and I'm not gonna screw it up on any level." And right out of the box, and again I think it smells because of the people involved, but still you cannot put your hands on students.

Even if you believe Knight's version, which I don't happen to. It's still too much. He still had his arm on the kid. He's still in the kid's face. I would bet you that he honestly believes he didn't use profanity on the kid. I guarantee you that he did use profanity on the kid.

Going back to when I was doing the book, the first question I was always asked was, "Will he have a Woody Hayes type ending?" You remember Woody Hayes, the great Ohio State coach whose career ended when he slugged Charlie Bauman, a Clemson player, during a bowl game in 1978. My answer was, "I hope not." But clearly, even though it wasn't on national television, this is that kind of ending. It's embarrassing. It's humiliating. Bob Knight, with his record, should have left coaching, to a standing ovation, after his last game at Assembly Hall. Instead he leaves this way, completely humiliated by what he has done.

This will be part of his legend. I think it's in the first sentence. When you write about Bob Knight's career, you have to say, "Bob Knight, the brilliant but constantly self-destructive basketball coach, who won three national championships but 'caused his own firing by grabbing the arm of a nineteen year old student, ...

I wouldn't be surprised if he coaches again. He desperately wants Dean Smith's record of 879 victories which he's 117 short of right now. That's why he fought to save his job in May, because he wants that record because he believes to be credited as the greatest coach of all time, which he thinks of himself as being, or close to it, he needs that record. I can see him doing television for a year or two. Every failed coach, whether they're failed because of incidents like this or lack of victories ends up in TV or radio, he would be very good at it. And I can see a big-time program on the skids hiring him in a year or two to come back.

This was a brutally difficult for Indiana. And even though I've been critical of President Brand for not taking this step earlier, it's still a move that takes courage because he is going to receive threats from people at Indiana who are still loyal to Coach Knight, and it's going to be a very difficult time for Myles Brand because he took this step.

What will have been Knight's greatest positive contribution? The fact that he always stood for the right things in college basketball. His players graduated. He never came close to violating a rule. He was always standing up and saying, "There's a right way to do things in college basketball and a wrong way." I've always said about Bob Knight, "When it came to the big things, no one was better, but it was the little things that always brought him down, and this was another example."

Which makes this an even sadder episode.

It's a terribly sad episode because a great coach should not be brought down by small things.

Actually, if you play that tape backwards, it looks like Coach is helping Neil up and showin' him on his way

Terry Reed

Terry Reed has watched the roller-coaster ride of his son, Neil, through stardom at Indiana University to banishment from the team and death threats following CNN/SI's expose of Coach Knight choking Neil Reed

This whole thing has just wiped us out. We're devastated; there's nothing we can do; it just keeps on. I can tell you from a legal standpoint it was very, very difficult first of all to prove that the choking or something like that—before the tape. By the time the tape came out, the statute of limitations was up. Legally, there have been a number of people from coast to coast try to initiate some sort of effort to see what can be done. Up to this point, nothing has.

Ever since he was a little kid, my son Neil wanted to play for Bobby Knight. It's a long story. Neil is the only person involved in this whole thing who has lost everything. Everybody else went on about their business—kept their jobs—making bookoos of money up there at IU, assistant coaches, a kid that wouldn't have got to play for three years got to play for three years—the (Michael) Lewis kid. Everybody involved, the AD, the assistant AD, who knew about it. Every single person involved has continued on with life in a merry way. The only person that it's hurt—there's no monetary gain, not any gain, has been Neil Reed. It's a sad thing. You don't know half of it—the blockage at the end there. It's like there's a wall up; it is over! It's an amazing thing. We've been through so much with this, and I know it needs to be out there. Every day since all this happened I get a call from someone, many I know in the media. Not a day goes by that somebody doesn't call and bring this up—not one day. Tell me you'd like to live that life—it's difficult.

Against Kentucky, the sixth game of his freshman year, he had an outstanding game; Pitino said some great things about him in Sports Illustrated, but we can go through all that. I'm telling you we're wore out. The Knight group, I'm telling you my son lived it. My son played up there. One of his assistants—the one who's suing him right now, Ron Felling, was like a brother to me. You can't get any closer to that program than we were; my daughter was his secretary when my son was a sophomore. We were living up there and she was a freshman. People don't realize all this stuff. Neil didn't even visit any place else; he was going to IU. It just didn't matter. You talk about, as a father, I'm a sick son of a bitch. I'm not gonna go and jump off a bridge over it, but this kid did exactly what I asked him to do. He didn't smoke, he didn't drink; he trained like a son of a bitch. He did every single thing and he went through as tough a high school situation as anybody—moved from town to town. Nobody ever said I was easy on kids but I didn't choke them. I don't hit them. And despite what people might say or think I might have threatened, I might have said a lot of things, but I don't do that. When Neil left IU, I was moving from Iowa State to Southern Mississippi. The choking thing was bad, but the slander has been horrible. There are some attorneys in Philadelphia looking at that. Hell, Knight ripped my ass in the Chicago paper just about a year ago—just ripped it—ripping at me. This is a long roundabout thing, but I lost a job over this deal. And he's raising hell about that and about me and how bad I am and he turns and fires his assistant two days before they play Kentucky. He's ripping my ass and he don't have his facts right. But he don't have to. You see Bob Knight doesn't understand the truth. He don't know the truth and doesn't give a shit. All he knows is what he wants. He gets away with it because he owns them—because he owns them lock stock and barrel. You rest assured, from zero tolerance on down, he told them you figure out what you got to say, but he owns them. He's the cash cow, and they're not running him out.

They always slander. You see, anybody who leaves up there at IU, they just rip. You cannot leave up there on good terms. You cannot. That's an unwritten rule. It's a good thing that Neil didn't have a background that was shaky 'cause had they had one it would have been awesome. It was bad enough as it is, but the kid didn't do anything. Anyway, on the slander thing, when he left up there, obviously if you think you're gonna continue to play ball you just have to bite your tongue. As a coach, I'm in this business, I also understand how powerful Bob Knight is, and I don't know if there's—you see I've got good friends, coaches and head coaches, at different places, and they said, "Well, this'll get him." I told everybody, including Ron Felling on the morning they had the big press conference to announce Knight's fate, "It isn't gonna work; he's gonna win it." Understand, I've got a little insight into this deal; he owns them, and when you own them and intimidate people like he does, there's nothing that can be done. We had to stay quiet. Now you try to prove slander—three years later. Now you've got a deal—where were you when it happened. The legal aspect, everything was wrong, maybe we handled it wrong. There are people now looking into the slander issues.

This has been very difficult with my family—just a killer. It has made it very difficult on our relationships. We've spent three years trying to nurture a kid that was so positive, so upbeat. You don't want to say—because it sounds like you're bragging about your kid, but how many kids do you honestly know that don't drink—train right. He did everything. One thing they forgot to say—this was the captain of Indiana's basketball team. You don't make the captain a bad guy do you, but when all this happened—the slander, you go back to that. But I don't know—it's extremely difficult. I don't know if it can be done—I don't know.

Neil has been approached about a book—even talked about a tremendous sum of money. On the morning of the zero tolerance press conference his literary agent got a call and said it was over, dropped it, and wouldn't sign it. I have no idea to this day what happened—nothing. I don't know. It's the same damn thing. Oh, I've got it all—I know what the hell's going on, I've been there.

Knight felt like he could do anything to Neil because—you know you sometimes feel you can be a little bit tougher to your own kid than you can others and he did. Neil took it and never said a word. If the big guys didn't rebound, it was Neil's fault; if somebody was late for practice, it was Neil's fault—he was the one who rounded them up and did everything. But the deal is, the first time, when threatened with this scholarship thing Neil Reed's the first one that said "Fuck You!" and walked out and that's why this has gotten so volatile and so personal between them. He walked out on Bob Knight. Luke Recker waited 'til Knight was out of the country and faxed in a transfer—how about that?

Now you got to remember, one of the assistants was like a brother. I was there every day. I hung around in that department, I mean in an unofficial way, and I'm not the only one, I can name you ten other guys so I mean there's no cleanliness there. The only rules they follow up there are the rules that Knight wants to follow. Do they cheat for players? No, not necessarily. They cheat for Bob Knight. They don't do anything that helps kids. Now Recker's situation—they went out on a limb. They couldn't afford another major deal right then. But like I said, Recker, when he did transfer, faxed it in when Knight was out of the country. Now that takes a lot of nerve huh? He was the only one, assistant coach, any of them, all the others. You know what they do when the assistants leave—they phone Knight or leave him a message to call or something of that nature. They don't do it face to face; they haven't got enough nerve.

Felling, after fourteen years, is suing for age discrimination and assault.

I feel quite sure it will never get to court. Can you imagine Indiana University allowing Bob Knight to get on a witness stand? Now they have got it into federal court, which means you've got a larger jury pool and you're gonna have judges that maybe didn't graduate from Indiana. But you're fighting in the state of Indiana, and it's gonna be a monster.

I'm stupid enough but I will admit I made a mistake. I don't know if you would say—worse than a false god or whatever. I always thought Knight did more good than bad but I'm way, way wrong. Now, does he do all bad? No. There are some things he does good, but I get sick of hearing them saying about his contributions. I've seen him twice contribute when he's starting to have a bad year. For them, and he contributes nothing—$250,000–$300,000. Well, you know what's going on in college basketball. There a lot of professors wouldn't have a job if they weren't contributing a lot of money. That's part of the deal. It's in their contract; they've got to give back a certain amount of money. Knight is their No. 1 giver. He's their No. 1 fundraiser—on a yearly basis. I know you're gonna have Lilly Corporation and some of the others up there, but I'm talking about individual givers. They don't have anybody. He always uses that. For a guy who doesn't want it to be a big "celebrity" thing, he does it at halftime of a ball game in front of seventeen thousand. So you see the irony in it. But look, it helped Neil, and he has given up a professional career—that's money today. I don't know. Neil's a good kid, but the emperor doesn't say he's sorry. Knight's not sorry. He hadn't even admitted that he did it. That's a test for him that means he can't take credit for it. But there's a twisted mind; he's crazy. He's vulnerable. Kids like that are vulnerable too. Neil, when he was there, and this is what happened every time. It's what happened to Alford, to Recker, what do Indiana fans like the most? Knight would bench Neil—take him out. Two or three times he won ball games for him after he was trying to be—course Knight will put you in when games are on the line. You know how hard it is to sit there under that kind of pressure and then go out and perform in the final few minutes? And he did it. And you know what that would do for him—get him deeper in debt, because the fans would go nuts over him. He was the little hero. And what it's all about was—this is why Krzyzewski's sideways with him—this is why all of them are. Knight's ego is such he will not share—his players can't be bigger than him or even close or on the level which is stupid 'cause they're not even trying to be. They aren't trying to be in competition with the man.

The first people that came to Neil turned down his proposal after reading—what is it you write when you give them your proposal?—synopsis or something because they didn't want to hear that—they wanted the negative and Neil said I'm gonna tell what happened. 'cause there was a lot of good up there; there was a lot of bad.

Everybody's intimidated. You watch the tape in slow motion. Felling slows but he kinda goes on. Now see, what people don't realize, the two kids that stepped up to the podium and said their thing—that they didn't see it. Well, one of them was guarding Neil, that was Lewis, so you know he saw it. The other was even closer. It was A. J. Guyton. On top of that, they said the coaches didn't break them up. For people who don't understand the video-tape—that was spliced. They cut out where the assistants had to go into it. It goes from Knight hitting him or choking him to Neil immediately starting another play. This is the way they splice game tape all the time and practice tape. That's my opinion. They accidentally left it on 'cause generally they go right back up to "on top at half court" and they go right into another thing. Well Knight goes and does his thing. Then Knight and Neil ended up down there at the free throw line on the other end and that's when the other coaches had to come in. But the coaches, in order to keep themselves out of it, spliced it. So I know there's some tape missing. So now Knight's deal was that Neil Reed even lied—Neil said they had to break it up when it doesn't show that on the tape. You can see on the tape they didn't have to break him up so but he still hasn't addressed that he choked Neil. But I understand and I know where it was and if you had to put somebody on the witness stand, they, too, would say "Yeah we did break it up." But as it is now, that's the only thing they can say that ever that Neil said that can't be proved or hasn't been proved. It can't be proved at this point in time without going to a witness stand because they took that out to protect themselves.

A lawsuit would get sticky because there's four people, Knight being one, who would have to go up and say they saw this. Now, Knight, you can believe this or not, has already given a "reward" or would you say "bonus money" immediately following this incident—all of them got raises. Now that's the truth. You see Felling's been fired half a dozen times and every time he got fired and come back, something would go wrong and here'd come a new washer and dryer; next time it would be a bedroom suite, or here comes a big screen TV. Knight buys his support and love. That's what he does. He don't say, "I'm sorry." You just get a new car. You get a new this. I'm talking about secretaries on down.

Knight, even in the face of the tape, he has refused to admit it. That isn't the only thing. I've seen crap myself; that's why I'm so sick. I'm the one who put my son at IU—what a huge mistake as a father, but there's nothing I can do about it; I've got to go on. I made a mistake. He didn't even visit Kentucky; he didn't visit Carolina and Kansas. He was going to Indiana.

Our whole family has gotten very little sleep for three years. There's a lot of nights where we're up all night long.

Indiana University is Bob Knight's University. He loans it to the University so they can have tailgate parties and some other times when they need it. It is not Indiana University; it's Bob Knight University, and I believe that now.

Bob Knight does not understand the truth. He only understands and says whatever he thinks fits. That's the way it is.

Knight finally said something good—when he said goodbye

Murray Sperber

IU professor Murray Sperber was forced to take a leave of absence from his teaching post in the fall of 2000 because of the Bob Knight furor.

Sperber has written the definitive books on the tenuous relationship between universities and their athletic programs. His latest release is Beer and Circus on how college sports are crippling undergraduate education. Earlier works include College Sports, Inc. and Shake Down the Thunder.

This whole thing is ancient history. I've moved on with my life. That's my position. I am a serious professor. I don't care what the perception is. I have a sense of what I do, and what I want to do with my life and one of the things that I really don't want to do anymore is talk about Bob Knight. I don't care. His fans hate me. Some people think I'm a great hero.

Sadly, his saga-and what has become my own small role in it-will continue. In the past, I have publicly criticized Knight's conduct, but nothing ever happened to him, or me. This spring, however, everything changed.

On March 14, 2000, I appeared on a CNN/SI television news report about Knight. Because I am a long-time faculty member on Indiana's Bloomington campus and have written extensively about college sports, the CNN/SI interviewer showed me videotapes of some former basketball players charging Knight with misconduct, and then asked me: What would the university do?

Knight has a history of questionable behavior. He has been accused of intimidating and abusing players and athletics directors, hitting a Puerto Rican policeman before a practice session at the Pan American Games, and throwing a potted plant against a wall in a temper tantrum at a secretary, to name just a few of the incidents. But the university had never reprimanded him, I told CNN, "I call him the Emperor of Indiana, and there is no one in this state who will stand up to him and certainly no one in this university who will.

. . . If you are the Emperor, you are allowed to do what you want."

Privately, I wanted to call Knight "the former Emperor." But I could not ignore the historical record of the administration and trustees' pandering to Knight, in their relentless quest to have a winning and successful basketball program.

The program aired at 11 p.m., and before I went to bed that night, I had received 14 e-mail messages, most of them condemning me for my comments. By noon the next day, the number of messages approached 50; most were negative, although a few congratulated me for my remarks. Faculty members sent the bulk of the positive responses, but-to give a sense of the tenor of such support-one colleague wrote in capital letters at the bottom of his message, "Murray, whatever you do, don't use my name."

The following day, Knight held a press conference on ESPN and denounced every person who had spoken against him on the CNN/SI report, including me. That prompted many more nasty e-mail messages, as well as telephone calls from newspaper, TV, and radio reporters.

My main point in the interviews? The *Chicago Tribune* quoted me verbatim: "There's a very well spelled out, very strict code of conduct for every person at Indiana University in authority: faculty, staff, everyone. But Bob Knight, because of his great fame as a coach, seems to be getting an exemption. I don't feel that's right. I also feel it makes the university look very bad."

Hardly a radical pronouncement, but it unleashed still more denunciations of me.

In the past, as a critic of big-time college sports, I have been involved in a number of controversies, but none of them ever affected my private life or daily routine in the way that the most recent one has. In fact, because of my scholarship on issues involving college athletics, sports journalists and others have frequently asked me to comment about Bob Knight and his antics. The recent occurrences, however, have pushed me into the spotlight-and into an uncomfortable and odd symbiotic relationship with the infamous coach-in ways that I certainly never imagined or desired.

Before the CNN/SI interview, I had made enemies, but no one had ever physically threatened me or launched ad-hominem attacks on my appearance, dress, speech, religion, or politics, or had spread malicious rumors about me. Beginning on March 14, insults along all those lines arrived in my e-mailbox, on my answering machine, in letters to the editor of newspapers, and on the Internet.

For example, at a Web site maintained by Indiana basketball fans, the "report" appeared that I never showed up to teach my classes after spring break! I had thought that I understood the frequent antagonism between the athletics department and its supporters on the one hand, and the academic aspects of the university on the other. But suddenly, in just the past few months, I have faced a steep learning curve.

Often the vilification has come from people who have no direct connection to Indiana University but are rabid fans of its men's basketball team and coach. In addition, the people who write letters frequently know nothing about me but assume that I fit their stereotype of university professors. Indeed, the most depressing element of the attacks has been the revelation that anti-intellectualism is alive and well in Indiana and probably elsewhere in America, and that although many faculty members spend many years in college towns, a segment of the local population detests them.

The daily newspaper in Bloomington printed a letter that stated: "After viewing Sperber on the CNN Enquirer gossip hour, It seems obvious to me that Sperber has never worn a jock strap. So the next time somebody . . . claims to be an expert of something they know nothing about . . . say that he or she is a 'Sperber.' Or, if you hear a child spinning a tall tale, you would call that child a 'Sperbie' . . . By the way, would somebody let Murray know that Staples is having a sale on pocket protectors."

In fact, I played basketball for many years, including two years as a semi-professional in France, but that does not make me more or less qualified to comment on the current charges against Knight-particularly after CNN released a videotape in April that showed the coach grabbing the player, Neil Reed, by the throat. I need only vision and a reading of my university's code of conduct to form an opinion about that incident.

In the wake of CNN's airing of the Reed tape, more journalists asked me for interviews about Bob Knight. I found myself on national TV uttering such profundities as "A university is more important than any of its sports teams or coaches, and it must not lose sight of that fact." Yet even that comment sparked controversy; many fans berated me for not realizing that the Indiana University men's basketball team was, to quote one, "far more important than the English department" or any other academic part of the institution.

Many fans also argued that English departments and positions like mine exist only because universities can support them with the profits from college sports. My first book about intercollegiate athletics, *College Sports Inc.*, demonstrated indisputably that almost all athletics departments lose money annually, and rather than contribute to the university treasury, they suck millions of dollars from it. But, alas, no one can drive a silver stake through the myth of college-sports profitability.

In recent years, I have studied and written about fan behavior, and I am very aware of its irrational component. Nevertheless, the best preparation for my current experiences was teaching George Orwell's *1984* numerous times. For example, in the original CNN/SI report, in March, Neil Reed described Knight's "choking" him and then said that two assistant coaches had separated them. But when CNN released the tape of the incident, in April, the tape didn't show the assistants approaching or separating Reed and Knight. I immediately started receiving e-mail from Knight's supporters claiming that "the tape proves that Reed is a liar-you don't see Felling and Dakich (the assistants) separating them." Similarly, in reading the e-mail from Knight's supporters, and also scanning their comments on Web sites, I have sometimes detected the same fervor toward their beloved "Coach" as the people of Oceania felt toward "Big Brother."

As Orwell explained, in the world of true believers, "War is peace," "Ignorance is Strength," and "Hate is love." College athletics produces strong emotions, but before my recent experiences, I never realized how antithetical the mindset of the sports fan is to the university tradition of reason, inquiry, and open discussion.

In an e-mail message to me, one writer commented, "Years ago, I heard an interview with you and Larry King where you confessed that you had never met Bob Knight. I find this disturbing. You would have people believe that as a member of the I.U. faculty, you were an authority on Indiana University basketball."

I replied that I have never claimed expertise on Indiana basketball, merely on the university's code of conduct. But the writer raised an interesting point: In my 29 years at Indiana, since 1971, I have never met Bob Knight, even though he arrived in Bloomington exactly the same semester that I did.

Like Larry King, many interviewers have asked me about meeting Knight. I explain that I have seen him in person only at games in Assembly Hall, the university's basketball arena. However, the premise of the query intrigues me: The interviewers are clearly envisioning a small college, or a bygone era, where the faculty members actually meet and greet the coaches. In the more than 40 years that I've spent at large, public universities, I have never encountered such a situation.

Nevertheless, in the 1980s, I attempted to meet Bob Knight. While doing research for *College Sports Inc.*, I tried to interview him, but I never got past his secretary. I did not take the rebuff personally-I had not yet published any criticisms of intercollegiate athletics, and he knew nothing about me except that I was a faculty member at Indiana University.

To this day, the question about meeting Bob Knight keeps recurring, and a number of years ago, it motivated me to take a poll of Indiana faculty members. I work in a nine-story building that houses many academic departments, and I went down the hallways, knocking on office doors and asking faculty members whether they had ever met Bob Knight. I had two criteria for my poll: first, meeting him was defined as being introduced and shaking hands; and second, the respondent had to have worked at Bloomington for at least 10 years. I polled 45 tenure-track faculty members, and of that sample, only one had had the opportunity to meet Knight, an English-department colleague, Chris Lohmann.

At the time of the possible encounter, Lohmann was president of the Bloomington Faculty Council and had been invited to a luncheon with university officials and members of the state legislature. Knight was the featured speaker, and according to Lohmann, the coach "made all sorts of denigrating and insulting remarks about the faculty. . . . I was so angry that I almost walked out." As a result, no meeting between Lohmann and Knight occurred.

The final score of my poll: 45 to 0.

Such an outcome prompts the conclusion: When and how would the average faculty member at Indiana University, or at most big-time college sports universities, meet a famous coach? Even a professor who studies college sports cannot easily gain access to a celebrity coach.

Basic geography emphasizes the point. At Bloomington, Knight's office was in the athletics-department complex on the far northern edge of the campus, a long distance from my building at the center of the University. The same symbolic and geographic separation between intercollegiate athletics and academics exists at many other universities. In addition, big-time college coaches are in the entertainment business, a very different endeavor from higher education. Those coaches often amass incomes of more than $1-million a year, whereas the average faculty member earns a fraction of that amount.

Finally-and my current adventure proves the case-power coaches like Bob Knight often regard themselves as separate from higher education-indeed, superior to it-and they do not believe that regular university procedures, including collegiality and codes of conduct, apply to them. Some of those coaches frequently say that they are "teachers" and boast of the graduation rates of their players-Bob Knight certainly does. But, in reality, many power coaches regard sports as war and believe that the end-or winning-justifies any means to arrive at that victory.

When coaches persuade universities to accept one standard for their behavior and another for professors and anyone else in authority, immense problems result.

Important additional questions also remain, most notably: How did people in authority at Indiana University allow Knight to become the Emperor and to do and say whatever he pleased? For the sake of the university's current and future health, the trustees should thoroughly investigate such questions and find the answers.

I was flown to New York recently by 20/20. They had originally wanted, and we're talking the fifth-rated TV show in America, to come to Bloomington and do a thing on me. I said, "Absolutely not." They wanted to come to our house and my wife said, "Absolutely not." They couldn't believe that anybody would turn them down. I guess in America where everybody wants to be famous, nobody had ever turned down 20/20 before. My publisher was upset; I did not give a shit. I just simply would not do it. What I agreed to do, mainly because my publisher's gonna send me out on a big tour, is agree to be a talking head, talking about college sports. So ABC did a piece about this woman at Tennessee and the academic fraud scandal there. They flew me to New York. We went up to Fordham at their football stadium. Now I knew these people are weasels, and my agent said, "These people are weasels, and they're gonna ask you about Bob Knight." I said, "yeah, I know that." And whenever they do I'll just say I will not answer that. And they did, they tried to work it in to Bob Knight a couple of times and I said, "Look I told you beforehand I would not answer those questions." So that's really my position.

That's why they call it "Done" Meadow

Pat Williams

Pat Williams is Senior Vice President of the Orlando Magic and has served as General Manager of the Chicago Bulls, Philadelphia 76ers and the Magic. Raised in Delaware, educated at Wake Forest, in 1967 he was the baseball Minor League Executive of the Year. He and his wife Ruth are the parents of 19 children, 14 of whom are adopted. Williams has written 19 books, his latest being Marketing Your Dreams, *an account about Bill Veeck, baseball's master promoter. Pat Williams starts or ends every conversation with a metaphor on life—even on his answering machines.*

Courtesy of Orlando Magic

Pat Williams

Let me go way back to the Olympic trials, Colorado Springs, 1972. I'm the GM of the Chicago Bulls out looking at the trials, and Bobby Knight had just taken the IU job. He comes over to me, introduces himself, we have a nice visit. He asks me if I would be willing to help whenever possible on recruiting, which in those days you were allowed to do. You could have alumni and outsiders talk to players or put in a good word or call them up. You were allowed to do that, I think up until the '80s, and then the NCAA stopped that. I got my masters degree at Indiana so I had an IU background. And we had mutual friends, so I told Bobby "Yes, I would be very pleased to do that." But it never took place—he never called on me.

The next time I saw Bobby was four years later—I'm the GM of the 76ers in Philadelphia—at the Olympic trials in '76 in Bloomington at the old field house. They had set up bleachers for the scouts and all to watch. I was standing watching a scrimmage and I remember Wayne Embry, who was then with Milwaukee, was close by. Bobby came—almost stalking—over and I turned as if to greet him, and it was, "These blankety-blank bleachers are here for you to sit on. If you're not going to sit on the bleachers, get out of

> *In 1962, NCAA semi-final, Ohio State versus Wake Forest, Billy Packer had 17 while Knight failed to score. It was Knight's last college game as he did not play in the title game.*

43

here." "That's just Bobby, you know," Wayne said as he was there trying to help me gather myself together.

Two years later in '78, I was invited to speak at a luncheon in Jacksonville, Florida. The Gator Bowl week was going on there, and they have a basketball tournament in conjunction with the football game. The University of Florida is playing, I think, Jacksonville. Indiana is one of the teams. It's a community lunch, and the basketball teams are all invited. The coaches are sitting up at the head table and Bobby Knight is off to my right at the far end of the table. I'm sitting next to John Lotz who at that time was Head Coach of University of Florida. The coaches are sitting at the head table; I get up to speak. As I'm speaking, Knight is there—I could see it out of the corner of my eye—he was reading a book. I deliver my address, and afterwards John Lotz came over and apologized for Bobby. I said, "John, what was that all about?" He said, "Well, I talked to him, and he said he wasn't going to listen to a phony." He said, "You sign high school kids—he wasn't gonna listen to you." Well, in 1975, we had drafted and signed Darryl Dawkins, "Chocolate Thunder," out of Maynard Evans High School here in Orlando, he was our number one pick. That was Bobby's explanation to John on why he was reading a book. We had signed a high school kid, which in Bobby's eyes was wrong. This was pre-now when high school kids are coming out all the time. Moses Malone had signed in '74, then we had drafted Darryl. This was not common, and this was Bobby's view. Apparently he was not gonna listen to me because we had signed a high school kid. That was over twenty years ago, and I've had no contact with Bobby since.

Who knows what and how the guy—tracing back into his past, and his roots—got this way?

Life's like a roll of toilet paper. The closer you get to the end, the faster it goes.

Hoosier Daddy

Clair Recker

Clair Recker is the father of Luke Recker, Indiana's Mr. Basketball in 1997. After two years at Indiana University, Luke Recker transferred to the University of Arizona. In the summer before his first year there, he was involved in a horrible automobile accident near Durango, Colorado. After a long recovery, he since has transferred to the University of Iowa to play for Coach Steve Alford. Ironically, Clair Recker has lived in Iowa the last six years and welcomes the opportunity to see his son play more often.

A Luke Recker story: On August 2, 1996, Alice Irene Girardot, ninety, lay dying in DeKalb Memorial Hospital in Auburn, Indiana. It was between 11 a.m. and noon when Marti Recker, a nurse at Memorial, realized the end was near for the beloved area resident who had twenty-one grandchildren, forty-four great-grandchildren, and seven great great grandchildren. She loved Indiana University basketball, DeKalb basketball, and Marti's son, Luke. Oh how she loved Luke. Was it possible, she wondered, to meet him? "Of course," Marti said, and phoned him at home. Luke was there and came right over. The tall kid was taken aback when he reached the doorway of the hospital room, for suddenly he realized the gravity of the situation; the room was crowded with hospital attendants and family members. But the way was cleared and he was ushered to the woman's bedside. She took his hand. It was five minutes before noon. "I'm going to be with you," she said to him with a smile. "I'll be watching you." She died at 12:13.

Luke Recker

I'm just nervous about saying anything at all because Luke's still playing and will still have to go up against Coach Knight. Coach Knight has his following of rabid fans who look at things from the perspective that Coach Knight is right. If he says it's right, it's right, regardless of what other people might say. Or even if things point to it not being right, it still doesn't matter. I think that was proven out when Knight was able to retain his job after the investigation. If that would have been me in my job, I wouldn't have lasted very long, and I can't imagine that anybody else would either.

I grew up in Ohio. I spent my whole childhood in Ohio and most of my young adult years there and when Luke was in the fourth grade, we moved to Indiana. When Luke was very young—preschool—he was already doing sports things that to me were amazing. Throwing a baseball, swinging a bat, which was the sport that I thought would really be the sport he would excel at and maybe make a living at. Right before his high school years, he made a choice to concentrate on basketball, after completing his eighth grade. He said he was going to start on the varsity basketball team as a freshman, and that was his goal at that point in time which seemed pretty audacious, and I said "Just be happy if you start reserve and get a little bit of varsity here and there." And it wasn't long into the season before he was starting varsity. He was no slouch. By the time he hit tournament time his freshman year, he was a very complete basketball player already—playing like a wing or a forward position, and I think it may have been as early as his sophomore year already, they were playing him at the point. He was fortunate to have a lot of good ball players around him. That's what he had always worked at—his ball handling. Even as a youngster, before he went to school, he was going toward those types of things.

As a father, I am exceptionally proud of Luke—obviously have been a Luke Recker fan ever since he was a young toddler. I really saw early on. I played at a small college back in Ohio, Bluffton College. Luke was just very good; it's hard to describe. I knew he was gonna be an exceptional ball player. He's a very good student, very intelligent kid, got a good head on his shoulders. He's got a sense of direction about him; he knows where he wants to go. He knew back in high school what his goals were—pretty far-reaching. He said in high school he wanted to play in the NBA.

Luke and I are about the same height—he's maybe a little bit taller.

In high school, Luke didn't really consider going to any other school but IU. The recruiting process happened so quickly with Indiana that it was just kind of a real quick whirlwind. Somebody evidently put Knight on Luke's trail and he saw a couple of tapes of Luke playing—never did come down and watch a game in person to my knowledge. After just viewing a couple of tapes said "Yeah, this is the kid that we need." Luke committed when he was still a sophomore. I think maybe that might have been the first time Knight was seeking a commitment from a sophomore. There were other players that I am sure he was watching at that time. As I understand it, the story is that Luke is the youngest player he ever recruited.

I've never talked to Knight very much. Our conversations weren't very long. The last time I had any communication at all with Coach Knight was the

Varsity is the British short form for the word University.

46

day Luke committed as a sophomore in high school back in '95. We had been invited to watch Indiana play Iowa, their last home game right before the NCAA tournament, and all the recruits were coming in on that day. But we didn't really know that Knight wanted a commitment. Luke was invited down as a recruit so obviously we went and saw the game. Indiana won. It was a fun atmosphere. We had great seats. It was something I enjoyed and we had a good time. We spent some time with Knight at that time. He asked Luke how he enjoyed it. Luke said, "It was great, we had enjoyed it." But we didn't know that the express reason for Luke being down there was for Luke to make a commitment at that point in time to go to Indiana. We didn't know that.

It came back to us, what's the matter, doesn't Luke like Indiana? They said he didn't commit. We said, "What's the deal?" So we went down two weeks later and met with Knight and his staff and at that point in time Luke committed to the program. We'd had no clue earlier that they wanted him to. We had no clue that was the reason he had Luke down there. We thought that he was interested obviously but didn't know how interested he was at that time. That is the last time I talked to Bob Knight.

There were other schools interested. John MacLeod at Notre Dame was very interested in Luke because I sent Luke to a basketball camp there when Luke was going into seventh grade. Luke wanted to go to camps before that but I had said, "No, your camp will be in the back yard." I had put in a real nice court back there and I said, "I think I can probably teach you as much as you need to know" because I not only played collegiately but I coached in high school; until I got out of education and went into industry. I said, "You just work out here and when your time's right, we'll send you." Then Notre Dame had a camp and he asked about it. I said, "Okay, I think you're ready for it now." Then he went and John MacLeod called and said, "Hey, your boy's a good ball player." I thought it was a friend of mine just playing a prank on me. Then when I finally realized that it actually was him, I thought "Holy Cow," you know. Notre Dame wasn't a real solid basketball school at that time but MacLeod was serious about trying to build a program and get them back on the track and get them back to the level of success they'd had previously when Adrian Dantley and Kelly Tripucka and Laimbeer and Paxson and those types of players were there. But it was close enough to home that when

> *Of the top twenty individual scoring games in NCAA Tournament history, only one name appears more than once: Austin Carr of Notre Dame. He has the top, three of the top five and five of the top thirteen.*

he left Indiana in '99 he thought he would at least be courteous enough to take an unofficial visit there. So he did, and he really kind of agonized over that a little bit.

IU was just a situation for him where Luke felt he wasn't getting the opportunity to develop like he felt he needed to develop to try to get to the next level. He could have had a great career at Indiana. I mean he had a great career at Indiana in the two years he did play and did very well.

If Luke would have been playing the off-guard for Indiana, I'm sure he would have stayed. I'm sure he would have completed his career out there. It was a matter where he really didn't feel he was getting the chance to develop his skills and Luke didn't blame Knight or anything like that because Knight was doing what was best for his team. And I don't blame Knight for it either.

After his freshman year, Luke went to Knight and said, "Coach, I want a situation where I can actually talk to you where I can have a relationship with a coach who will talk to me, who would say, "Hey Luke there's a game coming up, what do you think?" Or talk to me during the course of the game and say, "What do you think?" Just have a relationship you know. Luke said, "I really want to play guard. I want to get to the NBA. I made no secret about that when I came here, and I don't think I'm gonna get there playing small forward." So Knight promised him his sophomore year, he would give him a minimum of half of his minutes at guard so he could start showcasing or honing his skills as a guard. It never happened. It never happened. In fact it appeared that Knight was going out of his way many times to embarrass Luke with a situation. It was like he said "Okay, I had to agree to do it, but by God I'll tell you what. I'm gonna just show you the kind of man I am, I'm not gonna do it." Luke was still kinda willing to grit it out, but the thing of it is, it became very obvious from the reports we were getting back from people who really were concerned about Luke's future saying, "Luke, you can't stay. If you stay, you're going to . . ." I mean it's like Damon Bailey—his junior year. It was just like he lost all confidence. It was a lost year for him—he probably was in Knight's doghouse. Damon did have a good senior year, but by that time it was just like the pros said, "Hey," and they gave up on him. If you're gonna make the pros, you've got to progressively get better, you can't sit back there and have a relapse.

Damon Bailey played thirteen years in grade school, high school and college and lost at home only twice.

48

The information we were getting from sources that we know were saying, "Playing forward is not helping you at all, in fact quite the contrary." You've got to trust some people. These weren't malicious people. These were people who were genuinely concerned for Luke and his well-being and saying what's important to you. And it's not that Indiana wasn't but again if Luke was going to reach his goal, and again Luke's not shy about saying it, Luke wants to play in the NBA. He doesn't only just want to play; he wants to be a very good player in the NBA. In order to get to that level, he needs to start competing and practicing in a situation where he can really hone his guard skills and that just simply would not have happened at Indiana. So it was more of a business decision than anything else. It was a tough decision, a very emotional gut-wrenching decision because he really did enjoy his teammates and playing for Indiana. But by the same token it was just almost strictly a business decision. Now, unfortunately, that's the way college athletics are for players who have the capability of playing beyond that level. You've got to look at a situation that's going to be best for you.

Now there's a lot of players that will never have that opportunity. There are a lot of players who simply going to IU is a great situation for them—playing four years for Indiana, having four years of notoriety, probably a nice job offer when it's all complete. But in my mind, for kids who really aspire to achieve greatness, there's probably other programs out there that are better suited. Like a Duke, obviously, or a North Carolina or Florida and, hopefully, soon here at Iowa, that can get you to that level quicker.

At the end of his sophomore year, Luke didn't want to go through it all again. It was a bad situation. It wasn't too long ago that Knight had the number one recruiting class in the country. That's when Neil Reed and Andrae Patterson and Charlie Miller and all those guys came in. Andrae was the man, he was chiseled and stuff and Charlie was a good ball player. And by the time they were done, Andrae was sitting on the bench and Charlie was hardly ever getting off the bench, and of course Neil went someplace else. Richie Mandeville, another story, never got the opportunity. Were all these guys overrated in high school? I don't think so. It's just that I think Coach Knight tried to break them down and build them back up again in the way that he wanted to build them back up again and today's ballplayers are different in that regard. If you're a really good ball player, you've got to really think twice about whether or not Indiana is the right place for you.

Andrae Patterson and Charlie Miller are not bad kids. I met those kids, great kids. That's what they were—they were kids. I think there have been some kids who have had some real issues with that, trying to determine—who struggle with "Am I really as bad as Coach makes me out to be, am I really that bad of a person?" I look at the situation and think there's different way of conducting business. I've never been a Coach Knight fan ever. When Luke told me he was leaving after his sophomore year, I said, "Are you doing it for sure this time?" And he said, "Yes, I'm doing it for sure." I said, "Well, good." Because Luke and I had a lot of conversations and I didn't want him going to Indiana in the first place. That was his choice to do that. I didn't know at that time where I would have wanted him to go, but I told him, "Luke, you're going to be such a fantastic ballplayer, you can literally go anywhere in this country that you want." But being from Indiana and being an Indiana boy, basically he became kind of a folk legend at the age of sixteen. It's pretty hard to tell a kid when you're dealing with that kind of adulation from everybody across the state saying, "Hey, don't go someplace else." Because we all know what happened to Eric Montross when he decided not to go there. That kid was vilified.

On the website, on the Indiana Independent Basketball Forum, there was a statement by someone when Luke first announced that he was leaving IU that they hope he never gets to play again just because he's left their program (this was before the accident). I used to go onto it and read it just to see what people were saying when Luke was playing. I never participated; I was just kind of a 'lurker'; I guess is what they're called, where you sit back and read what other people have to say. Sometimes it's pretty aggravating stuff that they write and the only way you can respond is if you have a password and I'm not a techno so I didn't get into that. They said he did the unmanly thing—he at least could have faced Coach Knight and told him what his concerns are and tried to work it out. They don't know he had done all that the previous year, but that did come out later. Luke won't comment to that regard and I think that's good.

People who reside on this basketball forum are just Knight fanatics where Knight can't do anything wrong. But unfortunately I was reading the bad stuff; I wasn't reading much good stuff. They got an issue on there you are not allowed to say anything good about Luke Recker, you're just can't say it; they'll delete it. They'll delete the post.

It was not that Luke couldn't play for Coach Knight; it wasn't one of those deals like Neil Reed or Jason Collier got involved in. It was just one of those things where it boiled down to "Is this the best thing for me, in regards to my future?" And did a lot of things happen while he was there? I suppose they probably did but that wasn't the issue. I'm sure things happen all over the country and in different programs. It strictly was kind of a business decision for Luke to make and I think he made the right one. I think it was necessary for him to go to a different program so he could get himself ready to have a real legitimate chance to further his opportunity to have a career in the NBA.

I'm sure Knight had a difficult time when Luke transferred. But there again, he didn't communicate anything about it. I think for a while it was kinda sad in a way—I think there was some talk afterward. Luke, I think, was very gracious in saying "I appreciate the chance for playing here, and I have a lot of respect for Coach Knight," which he does. And he said "I have no one to blame but myself for my lack of development but I want to go to a program where I think I can develop better." Again in regards to Luke, after his freshman year, he really was considering a transfer at that point in time. And it wasn't a pleasant face-to-face meeting that he had with Coach Knight. He didn't want to go through a situation that was difficult for anybody at that point in, Knight himself, or anybody associated with the program so he faxed Coach his transfer. I know people really give Luke a tough rap on that one, but again they don't know what he had experienced the previous year. They said he took the coward's way out. But he just didn't want the confrontation and stuff because he knew it would be confrontational and that's not a healthy situation.

After Luke's automobile accident, he heard from a lot of people, including some IU people. Keith Smart called and talked to him. Luke's teammates called and talked to him. He got cards and stuff from IU. To say that IU wasn't supportive of him, that's not true. There's a lot of people from IU who were wishing him a speedy recovery. I don't think that any of the coaches contacted him but I don't know that that was a directive or not. He has a lot of fondness for the people back at Indiana and it was not anything malicious that he did. It was just him looking forward to the future and what was in his interests and frankly IU just didn't figure in his development, or his plans to develop as a ball player anymore. Because it was pretty apparent that he was gonna be relegated to a small forward position for his whole career there, and that would have seriously hampered his chances. He felt he really had to transfer.

Keith Smart's shot to win the 1987 National Title came at the very same minute that the movie "Hoosiers" was up for an Oscar. Keith Smart was an usher in the Superdome as a Boy Scout, the arena where he made the shot to win the title.

But the way it worked out, Luke decided on going to Arizona instead and really it was one of those deals where I was hoping that he would go to Iowa. Even though I knew he was gonna be not on scholarship anymore, I really felt, 'cause I went to both Arizona and to Iowa visits with him. It really boils down to they were both great coaches and both great programs. Arizona obviously was the better program, as far as talent-wise, but I really think that Coach Alford is going to put something together at Iowa and Luke could be an instrumental cog in making that happen. So anyhow he went to Arizona and then he committed to Arizona and then the accident happened.

After the accident, my son-in-law called me and said Luke was in Colorado and was in a bad accident and thought he was close to Durango. I had my lady friend get on the phone and call Durango to see if there was a hospital there. She got the hospital and they wouldn't tell her anything so I had to go on the phone, and they confirmed he was there. I had my friend call the airport in Cedar Rapids and had her get me a flight reservation at six o'clock in the morning. I didn't even—I just threw stuff in a bag and drove up and waited at the airport for four hours.

I had to fly into Denver, then to Durango so this was not an easy trip at all. I was there at the hospital in Durango when Luke finally woke up. A male nurse asked him at that time, "Luke, you need to wake up." They got him to awaken. "Luke, do you know this man?" Luke looked at me and said, "That's my Dad." Then he closed his eyes and was out for the next couple of hours. For the first couple of days he was only lucid for a matter of minutes—maybe fifteen-twenty seconds at a time. He absolutely doesn't remember anything of the accident and doesn't remember his hospital stay or anything like that.

Lute Olson was very classy. Luke has nothing but total respect for Lute Olson. Because Luke just, I feel pretty confident in saying that Coach Olson looked at the situation and, being the type of class person that he is, I know he really wanted Luke to stay at Arizona because he felt that Luke was kinda the missing link for another championship team for him. And maybe he'll still get one without him but it will be more difficult without him than it would have been with him. Really Lute is the type of guy that he put an individual's well being in front of his own fame and fortune, if you will. He said, "Luke's got to do what is in his best interests, and I don't think Arizona is the right situation for him in regards to everything that's transpired at this time."

> *The last ten years, the University of Arizona has the best winning percentage in college basketball.*

Iowa ended up being a better situation, and I didn't know it was going to happen. He called me and said, "Dad, this is what I'm thinking about doing." I said, "Well, I think that's fine," and I'm certainly appreciative of Coach Olson for going to bat for Luke and telling the NCAA that "hey this kid's been through enough. Let's don't penalize him any more by making him sit out a half season" just because he knew, too, if the accident hadn't happened, Luke would have been there.

It wasn't so much a basketball decision. He needed to get back to a comfort zone again and have some support, more emotional support than anything else. I have another child who plays basketball in the Big Ten as well—a daughter, Maria, a sophomore, who plays at Michigan State.

Luke doesn't have a scholarship at Iowa because the Big Ten has a rule that if you transfer within the Conference, you cannot get another athletic scholarship. I think it's to keep kids from jumping to another team in the Big Ten or having the opportunity to load up a team, I'm not sure. He qualifies to get in-state tuition because I'm a resident of Iowa and have been for almost six years and Luke's my dependent, and I claim him on taxes and all that. He's recovered from his accident.

Alford says there's no problem. He's never said anything. He doesn't want there to be a problem. I think part of the situation is that Luke obviously hasn't helped matters by deciding that Iowa was going to be the team that he would eventually end up with so that's not Steve's fault that Luke decided to come here

I think it's like anything else. It's no different than a lot of coaches. They're busy people. They're constantly recruiting and working on other issues so I don't think—I don't know if it's unusual or not. Do I ever talk to Steve Alford? Yes, I do. I just don't call him up on the phone, but I'm close enough. Last December, Coach Alford had asked Luke what he was doing for New Year's Eve. Luke said, "My Dad's taking me out for dinner at the Iowa Athletic Club." Coach Alford didn't need to do it, but he made sure he stopped by at the Athletic Club at least for a few minutes to say "Hi" and to talk a little bit. I'll be around Iowa City on occasion looking for Luke, and Luke will be out with the team playing softball or something like that which Coach Alford's a part of, too.

It has been interesting because a lot of people around here don't yet know that Luke will be playing at Iowa. We had a bit of a party here on Sunday. My girl friend sells real estate and she had some clients who had bought houses from her so we had them in. I was talking with a friend of mine and we were talking about Luke and this guy is a huge Iowa Hawkeye fan.

"Well it's a good thing we're about to football. Once football starts, basketball's right around the corner." I said, "Yeah, man, I can't wait. It's time for Luke to get back out on the court again and start playing some ball. I miss not seeing him out there because it's been a while." This guy said, "Are you talking about Luke Recker?" I said, "Yeah." He said, "Do you know Luke?" "Heck, yeah." He said, "How would you know Luke?" I said, "Well, he's my son." He looked at me and said, "Are you kidding me?" I said "No." I don't think he knew my last name at that time. Finally he said, "I can't wait till I go back to work so I can tell people where I was at." I said, "Well, you're in for another big surprise. Luke's actually going to show up with a couple of his friends, and you're going to get a chance to meet him." So when Luke came, the guy's eyes actually bugged out.

Cliff Hawkins, Luke's high school coach, is a good guy, too. He's been a huge support for Luke as far as somebody that Luke can actually talk to. In fact I think Luke thought that would be the kind of relationship he could expect in college, where you could actually call your coach and talk to him and spend a lot of time with. I know they still do that with Hawkins; he's a real good guy. Luke has a lot of respect for him and it's not just because of his coaching abilities but just because of his concern for his players. I wouldn't want to discredit Coach Knight or anything like that. He's like the Teflon coach; nothing will stick to him

I think Luke will do well because he's more mature and will be more relaxed. Not for anything that Knight might do or fear or anything like that, it's just that Luke's been through a hell of a lot. He had to grow up in a hurry and I think all the experiences he's had have not been all pleasant or all positive but they certainly, I think, have made him mature to the point where he can say, "I can deal with anything pretty much now."

I know you'll get maybe more information. I could probably say more, but again I'm not trying to assassinate anybody or anything like that, anybody's character.

Rodney King Probably Said It Best When He Said "Stop Beating Me"

Jose de Silva
Buddy Bonnecaze, Jr.

I told Bobby, "Hell, for 50 bucks, get the translator," but nooooo . . . he's a man of his convictions

Jose de Silva

Jose became famous as the policeman in San Juan, Puerto Rico, who arrested Bobby Knight at the Pan American games in 1979. He is now retired from the police force and is a lawyer in San Juan.

I was working that day because I was working security. I had been working since eleven o'clock in the morning, and this happened after one o'clock in the afternoon.

Well, what happened—it's been so long. Whatever happens, it's time the story be written with the truth. All these people, the politicians back in the United States they know everything that happened at the Pan American games in 1979. They know that Knight hit me. They know that he was extremely abusive in practice, and he punched me in my face. He did it because I called him over and asked him to please leave the basketball arena. The Brazilian women's team was there waiting to take the court, and it was long past their scheduled time. I called Mr. Knight over and asked him to please leave the basketball arena. He got my attention and told me he could continue to play, and the other people, the Brazilian women's team, could leave. His hour of practice was over, and he was using very bad language in front of those Brazilian girls. He said, "Get those dirty whores out of here." I remember, I said to him, "Watch your language because they speak English. Those people study in the United States, too. They don't need to hear stuff like that." That's what I told Mr. Knight. Mr. Knight said, "You take your ass out of here, too." I said, "Give me your name 'cause I'm going to report you." When I told him I was going to make a report, man, he just told me his name, and I looked down to write it in the notebook, and he hit me. He hit me with a closed hand that went to my face. When he hit me, I just jerked my head up and told him, "You're under arrest." I started to walk around the basketball arena. I asked him to come with me because, "You're under arrest." He said, "Listen, kid, get your hands off me, – – – – –." Because I had decided to mention him to the Committee of the Pan American games because that was the order that we had—to report things like that to the committee—the decisions that had been made by any participants of the games. So I asked Knight, and this guy first and this guy doesn't come out, and he hit me. At the time, I didn't know who he was—just a coach from the American team, but I didn't know who he was at that time. I know who he was after that and know he is Coach for the Indiana University. I played a little basketball and am a basketball fan. I was 34 years old at that time.

I don't expect it. I was writing with my head down, writing in my notebook his name, and I got hit, and he hit me really bad in my face. I had to go to the hospital. They told me to rest for a few days.

There were no other policemen there that day, I was alone. There were other civilian people around in the basketball arena looking for a place to practice, and they saw when Knight hit me and they called for more police because they believed that I needed some help there. The patrol came around and that's when I arrested him and put him in the patrol car. When I told the patrol that he hit me and I got assaulted, and Knight was arrested and Knight came to walk round the arena, and walk around and walk around, his helper, his assistant came around and told him, "Come on. The police say you have been arrested and let's go with him." I put him in the police car. I handcuffed him. He didn't fight back at that point. I just took him to headquarters and my commander called me and asked me what happened. I put him in the cell right there and waited for him to be in the front of the judge. The Chief of Police came to the headquarter to see whatever happened to Bob Knight and that was the whole story.

They told me to take him to the front of the judge to decide if he was guilty.

People here in Puerto Rico think Mr. Bobby Knight is a man who has no respect for the police, no respect for the Puerto Rico people, no respect for the human things—no respect for nothing. That is the opinion of the Puerto Ricans. He was in a cell by himself, it wasn't long, he wanted to take some bodyguards. I saw him again on TV that night. They gave him a chance to participate in the games and be in the basketball arena that night.

But before that he was bailed out and then the judge said he had to take charge of his team and he left him without bail with a representative and after that when the game was over, he left Puerto Rico. He never came back. He was in the cell in police headquarters about fifteen minutes

This other night, back in '79, Knight went to another guy of his home team, Isiah Thomas, he was a player on the Indiana team. When they were practicing in another basketball arena, Knight grabbed him by the ears . Other people were in the basketball arena that night; a representative of the team of Puerto Rico saw him doing that and said he picked really bad. In fact, Knight talked to Thomas really bad and picked him up by his ears.

I've been a policeman since 1966, and have retired from the police already in 1994. I'm a lawyer right now in my country.

I don't want to remember anymore that happens with Mr. Knight. I believe that somebody has to cut it out.

Then Coach Knight stuffed the accountant like a Thanksgiving turkey; go figure

Louis "Buddy" Bonnecaze, Jr.

Buddy Bonnecaze, Jr. is an accountant and investor in his hometown of Baton Rouge, Louisiana

This was 1981 at the Final Four in Philadelphia. I'm there with the LSU Alumni Association. LSU played Indiana in one of the semi-final games and Indiana won. It just so happened that the Alumni Association was staying in the same hotel in Cherry Hill, New Jersey as the Indiana basketball team. We go back to the hotel after the game and we're out on the porch having a couple of drinks and a couple of friends of ours came up, and I said "Well if y'all want a drink, I'll go get you one." So I go into the bar and order them a drink

And as I'm walking out of the bar, Bobby Knight walks in, so I just said one word. I said, "Congratulations." Of course, I had an LSU shirt on, so we just kinda pass. Then I hear this voice saying, "Well, we weren't your goddamn Tiger Bait after all, were we?" You know LSU has a cheer about "Tiger Bait," the LSU Tigers you know. I just turned around, 'cause the way he said it was obnoxious, you know how everybody calls him an ass-hole. So I said, "Well you are an ass-hole." We were about fifteen—twenty feet apart; he had walked on into the bar. He gets this mean look in his eyes, and he said, "You care to repeat that?" No, that's not what he said. He said, "What did you say?" I said, "I said you're an ass-hole." He comes running over to me. You know he's six feet, five inches tall. And he puts his nose about a half-inch from mine. He says 'You care to repeat that." I said, "Yes, you're an ass-hole." Course I didn't think the guy was gonna do anything. You know this guy Neil Reed that he choked, and then Knight said, "I never choked anybody." Well, I know he's a liar, because that's exactly what he did to me. He grabbed me by the throat and he shoved me backward and he squeezed on my neck as hard as he could. In fact, I went to the doctor just to document it 'cause I had some contusions all around my neck. I mean it scared me. I didn't think the guy was gonna hit me. And he just squeezed as hard as he could and he pushed me down and there was a big plastic garbage can. And when he pushed me back, choking me, the garbage can just kinda crumpled behind me. Of course, the story was embellished about throwing me into the garbage can. Luckily, there were a couple of Indiana assistant coaches who grabbed him as soon as he grabbed me. It was just about a second or so that he squeezed me, but he squeezed my neck as hard as he could. It hurt, and it startled me, and I couldn't breathe for just a second or two.

The reason he was staying at the hotel was a friend of his owned the hotel. So somebody from the hotel came up and started giving me a hard time. I said, "Whoa, wait a minute, I was just assaulted here." They said, "No, no." I said, "Well, I'm gonna call the police then. This is ridiculous! Y'all getting on my case about bothering Bobby Knight." So I tried to get an outside line; they wouldn't even give me an outside line to start with. I said, "If y'all don't give me an outside line, we're gonna really have a problem." So they gave me an outside line and I called the police, and the Cherry Hills, New Jersey policeman came. He got statements from several people there, and it was obvious that Knight had assaulted me. The policeman told me if I wanted to have him taken downtown and booked for assault, he would do it. To be honest with you, I didn't want to get my name in the paper and all that kind of stuff so he said, "Well, let's come into a room."

So the policeman, Bobby Knight and I went into a room. Knight was still just defiant. So we go into the room, and I had a couple of friends of mine who were attorneys who were on the trip with us. I don't remember for sure if they went into the room with us or were just outside. But anyway, we go in the room. So then the policeman is telling Bobby Knight that he had taken statements from independent people and they said that you assaulted this Louisiana man and I'm trying to see what y'all want to do. Knight just looks at me and said, "Do what you want to do." I came within a hair right then of saying, "Take him downtown." And if I'd have known my name would have gotten in the paper and all that, I would have done it, but at the time I said, "Aw, I don't know." We just kinda talked it out, and then Knight got a little more mellow as we sat there; we must have been in the room twenty or thirty minutes. At the end, he was more civil. He knew then, I think he realized he could get in a lot of trouble so then he started being a little nicer. Then he kinda got, "Well, I just thought you were one of those guys who were doing this or that . . ." I said, "All I did was say one word—congratulations."

The next morning it hit the newspapers, but the first ones I read didn't have my name in it. My wife and I went on a sightseeing trip that day, and when we came back, I just had a zillion messages in the hotel room, and my name was all over the newspaper and on TV. The local TV station interviewed me and several other people wanted to talk to me. I tried to be fairly low key about it and not get too involved in all of it. But just a zillion, I mean, every reporter in town wanted to talk to me, and I had a stack of messages.

Then, of course, we got all kinds of stories. Friends from all over the country—I got newspaper clippings from every newspaper in the country. Some of them were kind of humorous like "Two-fisted drinker"—that sort of thing. One of them said, I got stuffed in the garbage can but I never spilled a drop. All this kind of stupid stuff like that 'cause obviously that wasn't the case. The only thing I didn't like about it was it was almost like 'drunken LSU fan accosts Bobby Knight after LSU loses, or something like that, which was totally ridiculous. We had just had a drink ourselves and all I was doing was going in to get drinks for friends.

Knight had a press conference the next day and he said a bunch of LSU fans were outside their windows the night before hollering "Tiger Bait," "Tiger Bait." Could have been, I don't know, but I wasn't one of them.

When we got home, my wife and I have an office in the same building as an architectural firm, good friends of ours. They had a big banner put up, 'cause all those guys are artists, too, showing me getting stuffed in a garbage can. I took a lot of ribbing. I had to tell the story till I got sick of it.

From time to time, usually when Bobby Knight has an incident, people begin talking about my run-in with him.

I can't say I'm glad it happened but it has been a source of some humor in my life. Let's put it like that.

> *What Heisman Trophy winner has made the most money? The 1959 winner, Billy Cannon of LSU, was arrested for counterfeiting in the early '80s and spent almost three years in jail. Technically he is the only Heisman Trophy winner to ever "make" money.*

That's The First Time That Ever Happened Again

Steve Reid
Gene Corrigan
Rance Pugmire
Jason Collier
Peter Golenbock

A gentleman always gives up his chair

Steve Reid

Steve Reid is a footnote in college basketball history for the unlikeliest of reasons: He was preparing to shoot a free throw for Purdue early in a game at Indiana's Assembly Hall in 1985 when Bob Knight launched his plastic chair across the floor to protest the technical foul that had just been called on him.

Steve's father, Duncan Reid, is one of the most successful coaches in the annals of Illinois Prep Basketball. Seven of his former Rock Island Rocks played Division One basketball last year. Steve's brother, Bill, also played at Purdue.

For the last seven years, Steve Reid has done color commentary on the Purdue Basketball Radio Network. He is Vice-President of a Lafayette (IN) Trucking Company

What happened was I didn't see it coming. I had no idea the chair was coming. I had the ball in my hands and was going through my free throw routine and all of a sudden this red thing came out of the corner of my eye. My goodness, what was that—and saw it was a chair. I was just getting ready to shoot a technical—the first of two free throws at the time. The chair came flying across. The first thing that went through my mind was to go pick it up. That's one of the things my Dad taught me growing up. If you want to get "brownie" points with the officials, if there's a loose ball go get it and bring it to them and don't make them have to chase it down. My instinct was to go pick up the chair and as I was running over, I thought what am I going to do with it if I get it? Oh, probably just take it back over there. Fortunately a security guy was there and said, "No, we'll take care of it." As I was going back to the free-throw line, I thought that's got to be two more technicals. So that's six free throws. We've got a chance to get a pretty good lead here. That was the first thing that went through my mind. After that I got six free throws. I make the first two, miss one, miss the next one, turn around and Coach Keady is yelling at me—"Get off the line, let somebody else shoot." I kinda did one of these "No, I'll make these." Turn around and miss the next one—number five. The crowd is going berserk. I'm thinking I've got a couple of choices. I can somehow make this next one or I can miss it and go in the locker room with Coach Knight and watch the game 'cause I do not want to face Coach Keady. Next one went in somehow and that was it.

I get calls from friends every once in a while saying "you were on TV again last night." One called to say "you were on David Letterman last night."

I said, "That had to be the chair throwing incident." About three or four days after the game, when it had gotten so much coverage in the newspaper, controversy and everything else, I knew this was one of those stories that was gonna stick and be told over and over. I guess it's better to be remembered for that than for nothing but there's a part of you that says. geez, you play basketball from the time you're five years old and you're always trying to get yourself and your game in shape, and improve and be a good player, and hopefully do some things that people will remember you for in your playing and then in a matter of about five seconds, that's pretty well swept out the window because the one thing they will remember first and foremost is you being at the line when Bobby Knight threw the chair. I have never talked to Coach Knight.

My brother Mike has a great story. He tells it, I wasn't there so I can't attest to it, but supposedly Mike was a junior at Colorado at that time. Colorado was hosting one of the NCAA regionals there in Denver. He was in the coach's office and one of the assistant coaches was talking on the phone, and Mike goes, "Who you talking to?" The coach said, "Coach Knight." I guess he had called there to get some tickets for somebody who wanted to go to that particular regional. Mike grabs the phone and says, "Coach Knight, I'm Mike Reid. I just want to tell you I don't appreciate you throwing that chair at my brother." Knight says, "Well if I didn't respect the son of a bitch, I would have hit him with the chair." That's the story my brother tells.

The one reason I would not go play for Coach Knight is that most of the time by the time you're a senior, only one out of five seniors make it to that level without being in the dog house. It is incredible the number of guys who look great as freshmen and sophomores at IU and you go "Man, this guy's gonna be good." Then by the time they're a senior they play five to eight minutes a ball game. I think he mentally beats the heck out of them. Or he's also one who, like some bosses when they hire a new employee, think that employee's gonna be the guy who's gonna take that department and turn it around and make it the success that it hasn't been. Then, two years later, they're disappointed 'cause that guy's not doing anything right either. I think he's got that syndrome of guys coming as freshmen and getting a lot of playing time 'cause he sees their good qualities and thinks he can build on those. Then by the time they're seniors, there are some new freshmen or sophomores he's gonna give the minutes to. It happens a bunch.

Wilt slept with 20,000 women; these guys haven't even peed that many times

Gene Corrigan

Gene Corrigan is a graduate of Duke University who later became Athletic Director at the University of Virginia, then AD at Notre Dame before becoming Commissioner of the ACC. He and his wife are currently enjoying retirement in the Charlottesville, Virginia area. Corrigan was present at the press table during Bob Knight's famous outburst in the 1987 NCAA regionals. Knight's banging of his fist on the table and causing a phone to fly into the air became a celebrated picture in sports.

I was sitting at the press table. Bob Knight had just gotten a technical, which really shouldn't have been called. I was making the point that the thing with Bobby was he thought he was right whatever he did because he was wronged. It doesn't make a bit of difference what you do—he should have gotten another technical. He was yelling and walking around. He was on the court; he was everywhere—just kind of embarrassing. Finally he came over to the table where Schultz, Hank Nichols and I were sitting. He looked at me. He said, "I don't know why I got the technical. I never cursed; I never did anything." And I said to him, "You'd better go ahead and sit down and shut up or you're going to get another one." So that's when he got mad and he banged the phone. He said, "Screw them or fuck it,"—I don't remember exactly what he said. He did use profanity.

Then we fined him ten thousand dollars, and I was disappointed—very disappointed—when he appealed the fine because the basketball committee couldn't allow coaches to come over in front of the committee and scream and yell and bang the table. For some reason, he felt, because the technical shouldn't have been called—you could argue that it should or shouldn't have been called, and I felt it shouldn't have—he was allowed to do whatever he wanted. It was just kinda Bobby. He just never understood why we were doing what we did. I guess we were the first ones who ever did anything like that to him.

The fact that it was on TV and everybody saw it—the media didn't really do anything more than we did. Once it was seen and everybody in the world saw what happened, that Bobby Knight, the coach at Indiana, could come up in front of the committee and act like that, we just felt like we had to do something with it. At halftime, he came over and thanked me for telling him to go sit down. He said, "I probably should have gotten another technical." Bobby was—when he'd get mad, he'd get mad. He changed so much, though. Now it seems he always tries to put the blame on someone else.

I've known him for a long time; we weren't good friends or anything, but I was at Notre Dame then and he was at Indiana. Being on the basketball committee, we were with him a lot. I didn't know he had been considered for a Notre Dame job before he went to Indiana. I don't think he would have been Bobby Knight at Notre Dame. I think he would have been a very different guy. They wouldn't have put up with all that. It probably would have been the best thing in the world for him to have gone there; he would have gotten all this out of his way and just coached. I think all the things that happened with him—they kept getting worse because he was allowed to continue to act the way he was acting, which was in so many ways improper.

Knight doesn't like playing the late games, and I don't think that game started until close to ten o'clock. Like all games, it was two hours or more because it was on television, and this was the first year of the drug testing— not anything the coaches wanted anyway and so nobody was particularly happy with the fact that we had the drug testing. Then we went in a special room, and three of their kids, the three best players, Keith Smart, Dean Garrett and Alford, couldn't pee. They were dehydrated. It went on and on. I was concerned. So I called Tom Jernstedt at the NCAA and I said, "Tom, it's 12:30, quarter to one, can't we just let these kids go?" And he said, "No, we can't. You gotta go back there and do it," and while I'm out of the room, Knight goes in and I come back, and there he is sitting in the room (No coach is supposed to be in there. But think about it, it's really late. He's got to play the day after and he wants the kids to be able to go get something to eat.) So I said, "All right, out of here, I want you out of here now. You're not supposed to be in here. Get out." He did; I got his trainer or manager and said, "I want him out of the building; get him out of the building; nobody is going to be able to pee with him around." He's just so high-strung. We found out the guy conducting the pee collection in there was a Purdue guy, too, which made it a little bit worse. He got out of the room. So probably the whole team was in the bus waiting for these guys. Then they all left and went to get something to eat, and then these kids, within ten minutes after he left, were out of there. It seemed to me to be an hour—a long time. I felt really bad for those kids.

Ralph Floyd, the Athletic Director at Indiana, called me the next morning. Bobby and these players were supposed to be at a press conference at eleven o'clock that morning, and he said, "Bobby isn't going to come." I told him, "Yes, he is going to come. That's part of being in this tournament. That's what you've got to do. There's not going to be any excuses." Poor Ralph. He said, "Oh, God." Five minutes after eleven, he walked in with the players. I walked up to Knight and said, "Now look, I know you don't want to be here, but just go up there and be charming." He started laughing. He went up there, and for over an hour, he was terrific with the media. He was unbelievable. He could surprise you that way. I had never experienced anything like that. They were playing in the Hoosier Dome. The next game they played, I happened to be standing in the entryway when Knight came out and we were chatting for a second. Then I said to Knight, "There's 40,000 people out there and 30,000 of them are in red—the noise is just deafening." Whenever Knight walked on the floor, the noise got even louder. I said to him, "Coach, let me walk out on the floor with you; I want to know what it sounds like to have 40,000 people cheering for me."

He just looked at me with a little smile and said, "Gene, you'll never know." He winked and walked through the overhang onto the floor and 40,000 people went crazy.

In July of 1984, the first basketball game was played at the Hoosier Dome before a United States record crowd of 67,596 people. It was Bob Knight's Olympic team versus NBA Stars such as Larry Bird and Isiah Thomas.

The DOs and DON'Ts of dealing with Bob Knight—don't

Rance Pugmire

One of Bob Knight's most famous rantings—and most replayed on TV—was at an NCAA Tournament post-game press conference in Boise, Idaho in 1995. Indiana had just been eliminated by Missouri.

Rance Pugmire, now the Athletic Director at Utah State, was the moderator of the press conference and the recipient of Knight's tantrum. At the time Pugmire was the Regional Development Director for the University of Idaho.

Courtesy of Utah State University

Rance Pugmire

Boise . . . Let me try to remember back. Each school is assigned a volunteer as a liaison with the media room I had been the SID there for four years.

Looking back, it was an 8–9 game (referring to NCAA Tournament seeds)—one of those real close ones. One of the Simeon twins from Missouri tipped one in at the buzzer to beat Indiana. At the end of a game, you have a ten-minute cooling off period. Then the losing coach comes for ten minutes. Then the winning coach comes for ten minutes. The media come in, you have the sports comments, then you have to get them back out to the court to cover the next game. Then the next game starts approximately thirty minutes after the previous one

Ten minutes comes around—no Indiana. Finally the volunteer shows up and says, "They say they're not coming."

Locker rooms are open to the media after that ten-minute cooling off so I just made the announcement "It appears Coach Knight has been delayed. There is some difficulty getting them here." I didn't say, "Coach Knight refused to come." I didn't say that. I just said, "There's been some confusion

The NCAA did not start seeding teams until 1979.

68

and some delays getting here. But the locker rooms are open to the media, and I'm sure he would be happy to take your questions there."

In the meantime, I'm looking down the hallway, and Missouri Coach Norm Stewart, and his players are standing there and he is looking at his watch as if to say "What's going on?" So we get Coach Stewart up, and he makes his statement and the players talk. They're part way through, and I look down the corridor again and there's Coach Knight. So we excused Missouri. By now it's well past, way over for the time allotment, almost time for tip-off for the next game. I go down the hall to meet with Coach Knight and say, "Hey Coach we apologize for the mix-up. I'm gonna tell them It's our fault. We'll handle this thing." And he was upset and got after me then, and that's fine, it didn't bother me.

Knight comes up and I had made the statement, "We appreciate Coach Knight sticking around and coming. There was some confusion on trying to get coach and players out here, and Coach, again, we apologize and are glad you're here." Knight makes an opening statement. About halfway through, he turns and goes off on me, and I don't remember to this day what he said.

But I do know that I said, "Again, Coach, we apologize. If we could just turn our attention to the questions, please." He gets through another one and takes off again, and I don't remember at that point if he did answer another question or two and then away he went. That was the extent of it.

One good thing that came out of this though is that the rule has been changed. The winning coach goes first now, which works better. If you think about it, this would have to be the last game of your season, you're in there saying goodbye to your seniors. It's always emotional. Your season's over. We're going home. What are we doing? It's hard to get in and out of there and get your wits about you in ten minutes. Whereas the winning coach comes in, "Hey, great job guys! Let's clean this up. Okay, let's eat at ten, practice tomorrow at three, now let's go watch half this game. Way to go." They're in and out.

So now they've switched it. The winning coach goes in, and gives the losing coach more time with his team before they come in. So that's a good thing to come out of it, and that's the way it should be.

So yeah, Knight knew he had to be at the Press Conference, and Indiana was notified, but it's tough to do. I was SID from '85 to '95 and have had that experience a lot in a number of different sports and a number of different sit-

In 1985, the NCAA expanded the tournament field to 64 teams.

uations. It's tough after a loss to be in that locker room with those kids—tears are flowing and you're upset. The fact that he was late—yeah he was supposed to be there, and that's what the rules say you've got to follow them, but I'm glad the rules changed because it makes it easier for everybody.

When you look at the whole thing, the real error that was made was when he went off on me—twice—and it's carried on satellites all over the country. That's how high-strung the guy is; he's intense; he's very, very competitive. Did he need to go off? Absolutely not. Did I take it personal? Absolutely not. He'd have done the same thing to anybody else. Honest to goodness, it didn't bother me.

There's only one camera in there. Maybe the clips have been narrowed down to where there's only him in it, but as you open you see me and as you close you see me. If you see the whole thing, you can see me, because I got calls from my buddies all over the country that day, about ten at home that night. You know, people sitting in a restaurant or bar and look up and say, "Look what Coach Knight's doing. Oh my god, that's Rance."

I got a lot of calls; they were kidding me. I got a lot of "Hey, this is Coach Knight calling. Do you want to go fishing?" Or, "Coach Knight said to drive you off a cliff." They were all from different area codes in the country.

You hope these aren't the things Coach Knight is remembered for because he's had a tremendous record for winning, tremendous record graduating players and doing things the right way. Unfortunately, there's these other incidents that seem to take precedence over anything else you talk about when you talk about Coach Knight.

There are only five Division One schools without University in their names: Boston College, Georgia Tech and the service academies.

• • •

The rights to "Ramblin' Wreck from Georgia Tech" are owned by Paul McCartney. The rights to most Beatles' songs are owned by Michael Jackson

• • •

In the 1998–99 season, the leading scorers for Georgia Tech, Rutgers and Southern Mississippi were all former Indiana University players.

Notre Dame, Indiana, Georgia Tech.—this guy doesn't know what a bad fight song is

Jason Collier

At Notre Dame High School in Springfield, Ohio, Jason Collier was Mr. Everything. He was arguably the highest-rated recruit Bob Knight ever got out of his home state.

Collier played his senior year at Georgia Tech and was drafted by the Milwaukee Bucks and traded on draft day to the Houston Rockets.

The University of Notre Dame sued Collier's old high school for using their leprechaun's likeness—a tactic that didn't open a lot of recruiting doors for the Irish.

Jason Collier

I went to IU because it was basically close to home. My parents could come to see me play. It was just a good area for me to go and it was the biggest basketball place so a good place for me to go. I was recruited by Knight. At about the beginning of my sophomore year, a little bit at the end of my freshman year, was when things started to fall apart for me. I left there after my junior year. I read *Playing for Knight* by Steve Alford.

I remember one time when Knight came to my house on a recruiting trip. My grandmother, who is a no-nonsense kind of lady, grabbed his face—his mouth, shook it from side-to-side, and asked him why all those dirty words came out of his mouth. I'm going "GRANDMA!" Knight's face got beet red, and he turned and looked at her and said, "Well it won't matter what kind of words come out of my mouth, but what good things I'm gonna do for Jason."

The difference between Bobby Knight and Bobby Cremins, my coach at Georgia Tech, is "night and day." There's no pun intended.

Gee, where did Mike go?

Peter Golenbock

*Pete Golenbock saw up close what happens when a highly touted Indiana
player transfers. While writing a book on Jim Valvano and North Carolina
State Wolfback he got to know and like a young man named Mike Giomi.*

Golenbock has written over 30 sports books and has Mickey Mantle,
The Last Autobiography *scheduled for publication in 2001.*

Giomi had been selected Ohio High School Player of the Year in 1982,
and as sophomore at the Indiana University he had helped shut
down Michael Jordan and then hit the clinching free throws in the
Hoosiers' 78–68 win over North Carolina in the second round of the 1983
NCAA tournament.

Bobby Knight had dropped Giomi in the middle of the 1984 season, and
though he looked a little rusty, everyone at State was figuring him to be a
strong rebounder and an enforcer for the Wolfpack.

Giomi's departure from Indiana had been something of an enigma.
Giomi was such a picture-perfect forward that Coach Knight had used him
in his instructional films.

The official story on Giomi's departure was that Giomi had broken
Knight's hard-and-fast rules about how many classes a player could skip, so
Knight dropped him. Giomi had a 2.4 grade-point average at the time.

Giomi disdained talking about his experience at Indiana. When asked
about Knight, his usual reply was, "I see things differently from him, and I'm
going to be happy here."

One thing Giomi did comment on was the difference in approach
between Knight and Valvano. At Indiana, Giomi once observed, "Some days
we'd go to the gym without a ball. The whole two-hour practice was defense."
At N. C. State, it seemed that the only time Valvano practiced defense was as
punishment.

After reading *Season on the Brink*, John Feinstein's book about Knight,
a N. C. State teammate asked Giomi, "Man, how can you take that verbal
abuse so much?"

Giomi said, "You wouldn't dare grab him, because he's so fucking mean-
looking and he's big. He's six-foot-five, two hundred twenty. You wouldn't
dare challenge him."

The one story Giomi did tell was about the day he and one of his Indiana
teammates had played badly against Minnesota. Knight refused to let them

fly home with the team. "We had to fly back on a charter jet with the alumni." Giomi said.

Gee (Giomi) was a fundamentally sound, hard-working player. He ran the floor well and was tireless.

After one practice during which he was really struggling, one of Giomi's teammates had asked him, "Do you think Bobby Knight is checking the boxes on you?" Giomi said, "Yeah, he always checks on his former players." He looked sad. He said, "Coach Knight has seen all the boxes on me, and he's saying to himself, 'I was right about Giomi. I did the right thing.' "

Some of his more sympathetic teammates felt that the system had failed, rather than Giomi. "I knew he wasn't a failure," said a teammate. "Gee got ruined by Coach Knight, by Valvano, and by the NCAA that makes a player sit out a year when he transfers, even when it's the coach who forces him to transfer.

"Gee was a good guy, but he wasn't able to stick out four years of abuse by Bobby Knight, so he quit. And when that happens, it's Knight's fault, because he better know enough about each kid he recruits before he signs him to know he can pull his shenanigans on him and he'll still be there at the end."

"And then Mike comes to N. C. State, and everyone is thinking, 'He's a Bobby Knight product, he'll score thirty a game,' and he never comes close to that, and so the fans dogged him, booed him, called him 'slow' and 'flat-footed,' without remembering that he hadn't picked up a basketball in a year and a half."

"All he needed was someone to work with him. But Valvano wasn't the coach to do it, so Giomi was consigned to a seat at the end of the bench, disgusted and rejected."

Giomi's whole life would have been radically different if he went to a different college out of high school. Read the Mickey Mantle book when it comes out.

Hoops—There It Is

Dale Brown
Bill Frieder
Norm Sloan
Mike Krzyzewski

Personally, I think Knight has Post-ESPY Syndrome

Dale Brown

Dale Brown is a native of Minot, North Dakota and is the winningest coach in Louisiana State University history. He has traveled the world extensively and has written about it in various publications. He currently heads Dale Brown Enterprises in Baton Rouge, Louisiana.

Dale Brown

Tex Winter is one of the nicest guys in the world and he's now at the Los Angeles Lakers and was with the Bulls. He's in his late seventies maybe, and he used to be on a committee with Knight, and he would say "Knight always had to get the first hurt." Knight would come in and say, "Goddamn, Tex, where'd you get those damn clothes you're wearing—Salvation Army? They're shitty looking." Then he'd laugh, and people would go along. But, if you said that to him, he'd flip out.

I wasted a lot of time during the last decade doing something I really regret: feuding with Bob Knight. I should never have let the situation get to the point it did, but I'm glad to say that it is all behind us.

The first time we played against Bob was in 1981. We were in the Final Four and were playing them in Philadelphia. When one of the referees was running down the court, Bob stood up and said, "Get those guys off our back." The referee never said anything to Bob. The referee came down to me and said, "You sit down or you're going to get a technical." That told me this wasn't going to be a fair situation. The referee wouldn't say anything to Knight, but didn't hesitate to threaten me; I even ended up with a technical foul.

I just chalked that one up to experience. But in 1987, we played Indiana again. This one was for the right to go to the Final Four. We were twelve points ahead and the situation repeated itself. It all fell apart because everyone was afraid of Bob Knight. First, he got a technical foul for going out on the floor. Then he came over to former Notre Dame athletic director Gene Corrigan, who was at the official scorer's table as a representative of the

NCAA, and said, "You've got to do something about these blind bastards," pointing to the referees. Then he took his fist and pounded the phone sitting on the scorer's table so hard that the phone receiver popped up in the air. I looked at the NCAA people. They just sat there with their arms crossed.

I said to myself, "If I would have done that I would have been banned from the game. There would have been headline stories." Then Bob actually grabbed one of the referees by the arm before our player shot a technical foul. He kicked his bench, and the only reason the benches didn't fall over was because they were all attached to each other.

From that point on, those officials bellied up to Coach Knight. The rest of the calls in the game were in his favor. I went back and watched the film. Sure enough all but a couple of the next seventeen calls went for Indiana. On one play toward the end of the game, one of their players grabbed our ball handler and got a lot of body and a little ball. The referees called a jump ball. The ball went to Indiana. On another play, one of our guys got hit four different times while he was dribbling the ball near half court. They called him for five seconds. Coach Knight was later fined $10,000 by the NCAA, but Indiana went on to win the national championship in our home away from home—the Superdome.

I had a quick decision to make and my thought was not to shake the man's hand after the game, but just go on to the press conference. Then I realized I would be a poor loser. They beat us and I knew there would be a time and a place where we would get it back. I went on and shook his hand. I knew, however, that I had to do something about this. I went to the press conference and did not say anything about his tirade.

When I got on the team bus my daughter, Robyn, was there. She was very emotional. I said, "What's wrong, Robyn? We lost a game, big deal. We'll be back." She said, "That doesn't have anything to do with it, Daddy. What Coach Knight did, that was wrong. Especially for that old man." That sent a red flag up to me. I said, "What did he do?"

She explained it very thoroughly. She said, "I know he probably didn't recognize me, but when he came through the tunnel, he stopped and looked up into the crowd. With a diabolic look on his face he said, 'Hey, you LSU people. I stuck it to you again.' Then he turned to run into the dressing room. As he did there was an old man on the other side of the walkway. I don't even know if he was an LSU fan. The old man yelled to Coach Knight that he didn't think Coach Knight should talk like that, especially after winning the game. Coach Knight turned back and yelled an obscenity at him. too."

I took off out of the bus and headed for the Indiana dressing room. By the time I got down there, they were gone. I ran down the hallway just in time to see their bus drive off. As I headed back to our bus, Hank Nichols, the head of officials at that time, was coming out of a room. I called him aside and I said, "Hank, enough is enough. That conduct out there was ridiculous. You're the head of officials and you let him get away with that. Somebody's got to stop this man." Hank looked at me and shuffled his feet. "Well, Dale," he said. I interrupted him. "Don't give me that. It's the way you guys all start your sentences—'Well, Dale.' He's wrong and you know he's wrong." Hank said, "I'll admit he's wrong." So I asked, "why don't you say something about it, Hank?" He just walked away.

I went back and got on our bus, determined that I was going to face Bob with this. The next week at the Final Four in New Orleans, Bob Costas had me on his radio show and he said, "We understand you don't have a lot of respect for Bob Knight." I felt sure he was setting me up. I just said "Yeah." And Costas said, "Well, Bob Knight made a statement about you, too. He said that when Indiana was twelve points down, and it seemed as if he might lose the game, he looked over at the bench and saw Dale Brown was coaching. He wasn't worried anymore."

I said, "The way to settle this would be to put me and Coach Knight in a wrestling room naked and whoever came out first would be the best man. I'm sick of him bullying and kicking people around."

That made its way around pretty quickly. Then it got to be a name-called deal. He would say smart things about how he was not worried about LSU or Dale Brown. I would say something back. It was like two kids, and both of us resisted attempts by mutual friends like Pete Newell and C. M. Newton to get us together.

A year later, I was at the Final Four talking to Coach Bob Boyd. He was sitting at a table in a hotel restaurant and I was down on one knee beside the table. Over to one side were several of Knight's former assistants, Dave Bliss, Bob Weltich, and Don DeVoe. All of a sudden, I spot Knight. Man, my ears got red. I figured he was going to come over and talk to his assistants, so I would have a little confrontation with him. I was staring at him as he got near, but he wouldn't look at me. Knight walked by and he hit Bob Boyd on the back, but he did not say anything to me. I stuck my leg out as far as I could, hoping he would trip over it. I figured I would just deck him and get it out of my system. I looked like that old cartoon figure, the Plastic Man, with my leg stretched out as far as I could get it. Somehow he stepped over my leg and nothing happened.

Shortly after I hired Tex Winter, who was later an assistant with the Chicago Bulls, he told me a story. Tex said that one year he head tried to nominate me for the National Association of Basketball Coaches board of directors. Bob Knight was on the board of the NABC. He had mentioned to Knight that I would be a good choice for the position on the board. Bob said to Tex, "I don't want that cheatin' son of a bitch on this board." I got really mad. What he was saying was that we had to cheat to win, but Indiana doesn't have to. I had that in my craw for a long time.

Just as my disdain for him was really getting to be too much, a twenty-eight-year-old girl was killed in Baton Rouge. She was driving home and somebody threw a brick through her windshield and killed her. I was reading the story in the paper, and thinking about how painful it must be to lose your daughter like that. If that happened to our daughter, Robyn, I would probably become a vigilante.

A few days after the incident, a follow-up article was in the Baton Rouge newspaper. The police had found the killers. The newspaper interviewed the girl's father, a doctor by the name of James Upp. His wife had died of cancer prior to this happening, now his daughter was dead too. In the interview, the reporter asked Dr. Upp what he thought when he saw the picture of the young boys on television. Dr. Upp said, "Well, they certainly look like clean-cut youngsters and I have no malice or anger toward them. I am sure they did not mean to kill my daughter, and I forgive them. I only wish they could have met my beautiful daughter. I think they could have learned from her."

I read that story, and it just took everything out of me. I thought to myself that I wanted to live my life as Dr. Upp. I cut the article out and I was going to put it up on the bulletin board in my office. As I started to do so, I realized I was being counterfeit. I sat there knowing how much I disliked Coach Knight. I could not put that on my bulletin board as long as I had all that anger for him. That father could forgive those boys for taking his daughter's life, and I could not even forgive someone for something so trivial as our conflict. I put the clipping down on my desk and I opened the coaches' directory. I looked up Indiana University, and I dialed the number. The secretary answered the phone and I said, "Bob Knight, please." She asked who was calling and I replied, 'Dale Brown." I could hear her swallow hard on the other end.

Bob picked up the line. I started, "Bob, you can hang up anytime you want to but I want to tell you something. I want to tell you about an incident that happened here in Baton Rouge." I told him all about the girl, and then what Dr. Upp had said. Then I explained to him, "I was getting ready to put

his clipping on my bulletin board, but I knew I couldn't because of my contempt for you. I'm going to tell you right now, if I'm going to put this clipping up, I want to bury the hatchet with you. I want to forgive you. And if I did something to ask for any of your actions, I want to apologize.

Suddenly, it was as though the whole slate was clean. He said, "Dale, I'm sorry." He apologized for the incident that had upset Robyn. He said, "I appreciate your call and I want to bury the hatchet. Maybe we can work on a friendship." From that day on it was as if a cross was lifted off my back because I'm not a hateful person.

A year later, I tried to reach out again, calling Indiana and offering Bob's son a scholarship to LSU after Bob suspended him from the team.

Calling him was one of the hardest things I have ever done. First of all, I didn't know what I would receive from the other end. And I wasn't humble enough to do that naturally. I'm sorry that it took a death to teach me that lesson. But anger and hatred only weigh you down and kill a part of you. By hating, you are really losing twice.

There's a difference between religion and spiritualism so I've always tried to be spiritual and do what was right. I do a lot of corporate speaking and one of the parts of my speech is that being a human being is so complicated that none of us can get it right and we're living under the false impression that God wants perfection. He doesn't. All he wants from us is to do our best and never give up—never give up, and he'll take care of the rest. You grow into spiritualism, too, I think you think you're more spiritual than you are. When you get out of the arena, you then look back and have more time to concentrate and ponder things.

The most powerful probing answer about, "What'd you think about Bob Knight getting fired?" came from Krzyzewski. He used one word—remember what it was? It was "tragic." And I think in that one word he was including Knight in it. Tragic how he acted. Tragic what happened to him. Tragic the Indiana situation. I think that was probably the most probing thing with only one word describing the situation but I don't think there's any question he needs help, and he'll probably never get it.

When the NCAA calls,
ya gotta accept the charges

Bill Frieder

After an outstanding high school coaching career in Saginaw and Flint, Michigan, Frieder joined Johnny Orr's staff at the University of Michigan in 1973. He became head coach and put together Michigan's 1989 NCAA Champions before leaving for Arizona State. After Athletic Director Glen Schembechler was told Frieder was going to the Valley of the Sun, he wouldn't allow Frieder to coach the Wolverines in the Final Four. After being forced out at ASU in 1997, Frieder runs an investment company in Paradise Valley, Arizona. He is banned from most casinos around the world because of his extraordinary ability in playing Blackjack.

People make too big a deal out of Bobby Knight. You'd think he was the only coach, or maybe the only person, in the league. Whatever Bobby's doing is always the biggest news in the Big Ten. The only thing that comes close is what his team is doing.

The fans at Michigan's Crisler Arena were always their loudest and most involved for Michigan's games with Indiana. And whose face was on the Midwest editions of all the pre-season magazines? They even had a full page ad for some investment company or something, half of which was a picture of him, in our own Michigan basketball program! I told our people to get it out of there.

I don't agree with everything Dale Brown says, but the former Louisiana State coach was right when he said Bobby tries to get his way by intimidating people—referees, other coaches, his players. Mort, my friend, says this is because he's (Bobby and Mort both, really) an only child and a Scorpio and that's the way they are. Mort pays attention to that kind of stuff; I don't. It wasn't gonna help me win games.

Maybe it's only the media that make too big a deal out of Bobby. With them, it's more like a manipulation. He gets his tail beat but the whole story is not the game. The whole story is something else, and then nothing happens to him. I saw that for fifteen years.

I remember Iowa was beating him in Bloomington one year and the whole story was about Wayne Duke and the officials. It was the game where he went to Wayne during one of the timeouts and ripped Wayne on the officials.

He picked that fight with me in 1984 after I beat him, or I should say my team beat his team—see how easy it is to fall into that, and here we go again. Here he was getting beat and the whole story is whether he did me a favor and his breaking into my press conference, and nothing about my players winning a great basketball game. They were young kids, and they had no business beating Indiana that day, but that's Bobby Knight.

And that's always what it seems to come down to. We beat Indiana in Bloomington by 12 points one season and the story was how this was Bobby's worst start ever at Indiana and the program was in ruins and "What's Wrong with the Hoosiers?" and all this bull.

Mort says Hank Hersch of *Sports Illustrated* told him that Knight is like the pivot that the league revolves around. Coaches are judged on how often they beat Knight, or whether they're pro-Knight or anti-Knight, and so on.

And, sure enough, after we beat them again, this time by 20 in Ann Arbor, the story was how I was now 8–8 against Bobby and I had won five of my last seven against Bobby and I had swept Bobby for the second time in three seasons. See? It was like now I was a good coach because I was .500 against Bobby.

Bobby liked me just fine when his teams were beating mine all the time. The trouble started when my teams started beating his. He and Johnny Orr were supposedly such great friends, but you notice Bobby beat Orr's butt more than Orr beat his. Now they're still great friends, but they don't play each other, either, do they? I don't think Bobby has too many friends among the coaches he plays regularly.

Some people say he just loses control of himself but I don't agree. He's setting the agenda and it's calculated. This man knows what he's doing. I don't think Bob Knight has ever lost control.

It's a fact that the Big Ten isn't going to discipline him, and neither is the NCAA. But what would happen if you worked for The University of Michi-

> *Big Ten Commissioner Wayne Duke and John "Duke" Wayne were once Co-Grand Marshals of the Rose Bowl Parade. The Rose Bowl Parade had nothing to do with roses. It was to cele-brate the end of the orange-picking season.*
>
> • • •
>
> *Johnny Orr is the winningest basketball coach in the history of two schools: Michigan and Iowa State University. Bear Bryant, Dick Tomey and George Welsh have accomplished the same feat in college football.*

gan or Arizona State and you threw a chair, or hit a policeman, or pulled your team off the floor? I'll tell you what, you wouldn't do it again. If you were lucky, you might get one warning, but I doubt it. How did it come about that Knight and I had a falling out?

It's funny that incident with him ever happened. If we'd had the coaching box back then, it probably wouldn't have. I would have had to work another official to get that other official to do what he had to do. I never would have gotten close enough to him for him to hear, or think he heard, what I said.

Even at that, there were a lot of coincidences involved.

First, there was the fact that I was at Crisler the Friday morning before the Indiana game, which was on a Saturday afternoon. We had lost to Ohio State, a team that hadn't won a game in the Big Ten up until then, at the buzzer Thursday night, so I didn't go to the office at all. I was at Crisler until five or six in the morning, might have gone home for a couple of hours, then went right back. Now maybe in another situation, I wouldn't have been at the arena at 11 in the morning, but I was.

Second, Indiana had played at Michigan State Thursday night, so they were there for like a noon practice. Normally, it's 5:30.

And third, John Viges of the *Ann Arbor News* shows up. So for this whole situation to happen required an unusual sequence of events. Usually I would come a little later, usually they would practice later, and usually Viges wouldn't be there, but it all happened.

So I walked out to say hello to Knight and Viges was out there. This was when Knight wasn't talking to anybody in the media, and Viges asked me if I could get him an interview with Bob. He must have found out somehow that they were practicing at noon, so he came over.

So I went out and Bob and I sat on the scorer's table. We got talking and I said, "Bob, they're on my butt because I didn't start Tim McCormick." Viges ripped me for not starting McCormick and the *Daily* ripped me for playing him 28 minutes because I knew he was sick.

McCormick hadn't been playing well. He got one rebound the game before Ohio State. So I said, "Yeah, they're rippin' my butt for changing the lineup."

He said, "Well, I've changed the lineup 17 different times already this year. What the hell has that got to do with it?"

I said, "Well, my guy's out there right now. He wants to interview you. Why don't you talk to him about it?"

He said, "I will."

That was it. That was the favor, okay? That was the favor I asked of him. He said, "What kind of guy is he?"

I said, "He's a good guy. I want you to do the interview with him." So that was the favor.

Now, during the game, he was up berating the officials; intimidation, like he always does. None of that bothered me, except that my guy was waiting to shoot a free throw, and we're waiting and we're waiting and we're waiting for the referee and Knight to finish their conversation.

Finally, I said, "Either sit the SOB down or give him a technical." Probably five or ten seconds before I said that, the Ref had given him a technical, but I didn't know that. I must have been looking back at our end of the floor to see what was going on. Whatever it was, I didn't see it.

Knight claims that I said, "give him another technical," which I didn't, but it doesn't really matter what I said because he shouldn't have been taking up the time. We should have been playing. Let the kids decide the game, not him.

Then Knight came after me, calling me a chicken-bleep SOB and that kind of stuff.

He chewed me out all the way into the tunnel at halftime, calling me every name in the book, just like I read he calls his players. My biggest thing then, when I walked in-we were four ahead at the half-was, hey, we're gonna win this game. We are not letting his commotion detract from what we've got to do as basketball coaches. We did a great job in that locker room, putting all this behind us and coaching our team, instead of going in there bitching and complaining about Bobby Knight, which is what he probably wanted.

It's the same old thing. Bob Knight, if he gets beat, he wants to find a way to distract from his loss. Purdue's beating him, he throws a chair. Michigan beats him, he does something else. The Russians are beating him, he pulls his team off the floor. So that when he gets his tail beat and walks into a press conference, the story isn't the game, the story is what Bob Knight did, the story is some of his antics, and that's what happens all the time.

I started off the press conference by asking for a vote on throwing out Jim Spadafore of the *Detroit News* because he had written a story misquoting my players. I wasn't really serious-Spad's a good guy and I just wanted to have some fun with him-but I like to keep the press a little off balance and I wanted to relieve the mood.

I didn't even know there was a back door to the room where we have the press conferences at Crisler, but during the vote Knight storms in. It was

quite a shock because like I said, Knight wasn't talking to the press then, or going to press conferences.

Well, he not only came to this one, but he also started off by making some sarcastic remark about how he didn't like to hear the media criticized. I said I hadn't realized Bobby was there and I'd let him talk and come back later. And then he laid into me, calling me more (but not very different) names, saying I had used him, talking about how much he had done for me, and so on. Lynn Henning, who was covering my team then for the *Detroit News,* wrote that "to anyone there, the whole ugly scene felt like a punch in the stomach." That covers it pretty well.

After he was finished and I came back, they all wanted to talk about Bob Knight. No one wanted to talk about the job my basketball team did in beating Indiana when they had lost by 27 points in Bloomington the year before.

When I got home that day, I told Janice, my wife, "You know, this is so ridiculous. As badly as I feel, and as upset as this guy has got me, I wish we'd have lost the game. You shouldn't have to go through something like this."

I honestly felt that. I felt that, hey, I don't want to go through this nonsense. If you can't compete against each other and then be friends afterwards, then who needs it? I was upset because I thought the guy was a friend, and a friend does not act that way.

He called me at my house that night. He called me at my house the next day. I didn't even want to talk to him, but I did, and I tried to defend myself. You could see that he was upset, that he was not going to bed, that he thought I was entirely wrong and disloyal or whatever. I think he wanted an apology.

He was upset at some of the things I said at the press conference, I forget exactly what. He said I lied to the press. I tried not to discuss it, but he had on tape everything that I said. He was upset that I did not admit that he did me a favor, that was the crux of it. We just kind of got into it again, so it just never got settled.

I don't remember ever calling him after that. I answered his calls a couple of times within the next year or so, but I didn't talk to him at the press conferences and meetings. We really haven't talked since then, and that's fine with me.

He did get a hold of me after many attempts in Charlotte at the NCAA tournament in '87 because my manager screwed up and said I was there after I had not taken the call. He wanted to congratulate me for beating Purdue. I was going to prove to the world that I don't need favors from him to have a successful program.

He's the type of guy who, when this happened, called everybody. Everybody. He called coaches. He called media people. He called mutual friends. He wanted to tell them his side of the story and get their support.

I never called anybody to discuss the matter but when I would run into a Sparky Anderson—"Oh, Bob Knight called me"-or if I'd run into a coach-"Hey, Bob Knight called me about this." He called everybody, because now he's trying to get support and justify what he did. I think if he did do me a favor, it's not a favor when you call a press conference and talk about it.

If I do anything for anybody, they can stab me in the back but then I don't go tell other people what I did for them. If I do somebody a favor, it's a favor, and it's over.

I made a mistake my third year as head coach when I let him come into my locker room and talk to my team. It seemed like a nice thing at the time because I had great respect for the man, but I would never have allowed it to happen if I knew he was going to call a press conference and tell about it.

He said, "I can't believe Frieder did this to me, when I went into his locker room and talked to his team one time."

Former coach, Jim Dutcher, told me after I did that that I made a mistake. He said, "You should never have let him go in there, because you'll owe him. You'll owe him the rest of your life because he thinks he did you a big, big favor. You're as good as basketball coach as he is. You don't need him."

What it amounts to is, he's your friend as long as he beats your butt every time you compete. And as soon as you start beating him, you're no longer his friend. At least, that's how it was with me.

Knight and I had a great relationship before that incident. I first met him when we were on clinics together when I won the state championship at Flint Northern and he first went to Indiana, which was 1971 or '72. Then I came to Michigan in '73. I always respected him. I always thought he was the finest coach in the country. I knew he was doing a great job. He knew that I liked him, that I was observant of what Indiana basketball was accomplishing and how they were accomplishing it, and that I was trying to learn from him.

You know, we had Orr's 50th birthday party and Janice, my wife, invited Knight and he came. I don't think he'd have come to many assistants' houses.

When we went to Bloomington, Janice went over to their house. We had a pretty good friendship going. When the game was over, he'd be patting me on the back, telling me how my kids were coming along, and to hang in there, we're getting better.

Knight paid me a great compliment once, and maybe that's why he got so upset with me. He sent me a picture of the two of us at the national championship in Philly in 1981 from when I went down and wished him good luck before the game. In fact, they were all amazed that I could get down there, because I didn't have any pass or anything.

Then somehow there was a picture taken of it, of me wishing him good luck before the game. So he got it laminated and wrote on it. "Some day the positions will be reversed" or something like that.

In all honesty, that' a great compliment-isn't it?-from a great coach when I'm a first-year coach. I don't think he would do that for too many people. Now because of all that, maybe he felt that I was in a special category of one of his lieutenants or whatever. I think that's what he imagined. Now all of a sudden these incidents come up and it's something that he can't take because he thinks he's been betrayed. Maybe he's going back to the war or something and he's been betrayed by one of his men, and he can't cope with that. I think that's what he went through with it all, and that wasn't the case at all. I was just trying to win a basketball game.

I think our relationship would probably still be good today if he had just called me afterward and said, "Hey, I think you made a mistake. I'm talking to the official and you shouldn't interfere when I'm talking to the official." I would have agreed with him then. I'm an easy guy to get along with.

He's accomplished too much, but if the United States had the guts to let him coach in the Olympics and nothing happened, maybe he'll make it. What guts that took, huh? And they stood by him, but thank God he won. Thank God something didn't happen where he was getting beat and there was some bad incident.

You can tell by his book (*Season on the Brink*) that he doesn't like me or Michigan. What poetic justice it was to beat him in the first Big Ten game of the 1986 season. Going into that game, he's telling his team we haven't played anybody, and our last nonconference game was who? Cleveland State, who beats them in the first round of the NCAA tournament. I never thought I would see the day when Knight didn't respect opponents, but evidently he didn't respect Cleveland State if he would tell his team we hadn't played anybody and we're fat and lazy.

What an honor it was for me and my team that he prepared for Michigan during his Christmas tournament. That's in the book, about how he didn't worry about San Jose State and all of them, he worried about Michigan, prepared for Michigan, and then we beat 'em down there. That was satisfying, if he put that much into the game.

But see, then he lost the next game to Michigan State. That's what happens if you put too much effort into one game. You cannot do that at that level, and he made a serious mistake there. It was extremely important to me to get the best kids in Michigan to commit to Michigan. I thought that was a real weakness in the program when I took over, that there wasn't a single Michigan kid on the team, but do you notice how few Indiana kids there were in Knight's program near the end? Part of the reason for that is the jaycees he's taking.

That shows there's a lot of two-face in Bobby Knight. When I was an assistant, you cannot believe how he ripped the schools that were taking jaycees (Junior College transfers). How they cheat. How he will never take a jaycee kid because they've got bad attitudes. How there's a reason that they're in junior college, that they can't do the work academically. He went on and on and on, but he went and got jaycees when he had a bad season.

Well, what kind of person is that? He compromised. I don't like people who compromise their principles. And then he wins the national title and he goes out and gets more jaycees. It's almost like once he acquired the taste, he forgot about his principles.

Also in *Season on the Brink* is a scene where Indiana is playing Iowa at home and the referees give George Raveling a technical. Knight comes over and asks them to give him another technical.

That's the same thing he said I did that got him irritated, and it's another example that if Bobby Knight decides to do it, it's okay, but if someone else decides to do it, you're violating the code. It's just like the jaycees. If someone else takes jaycees, it's not good, but if he takes 'em, then it's okay.

And don't ever let him tell people that Michigan fans are the worst because his fans haven't been that nice to me, even though I entertained 2,000 of them in New Orleans at the national finals in '87 when I saw them up and down Bourbon Street. They were all shaking my hand and being nice to me because we beat Purdue for them to give 'em the co-championship and the number one seed. I mean, I just set the whole national championship up for them.

All those fans were nice to me and promised me a standing ovation in Bloomington, and I did get some cheers when I got introduced that next year—I think it was my boys I met on Bourbon Street-but when I go off that court, I get stuff thrown at me. I hear 'em talking.

How's he think the people are gonna treat him when he walks out there after the way he acted? You know what I mean? What the hell does he expect?

May the best team win and your team lose

Norm Sloan

Norm Sloan led the North Carolina State Wolfpack to the 1974 NCAA title. The Wolfpack were led by David Thompson, Tom Burleson, and Monte Towe. Sloan now is enjoying retirement in Newland, North Carolina.

Bobby Knight doesn't want to be called Bobby any longer, sort of like when Lefty Driesell wanted to be called Charles. It didn't work, and he finally gave up. Bobby may get upset about it, but he's still "Bobby" to me. I don't mean any disrespect, but he's been Bobby all of his life, and suddenly he thinks that isn't proper and wants to be called Bob.

You're going to get along fine with Bobby Knight until you recruit against him and beat him, until you compete against him and beat him, or if you ever have the audacity to challenge him on any of his regular pronouncements.

I am fortunate in that I have a wonderful marriage. I married a marvelous woman, a tough lady whom I respect immensely. I would no more demean her in public than I would sprinkle salt and pepper on Michael Jordan's sneakers and try to eat them.

We had breakfast with Bobby and his first wife in the coffee shop of one of the big Las Vegas hotels while we were at the Pizza Hut Classic in the mid-seventies. Joan and I came away from that breakfast with queasy stomachs. Bobby had demeaned his wife over breakfast, talking down to her and about her in front of her so viciously that both of us were stunned.

Later, we were playing in the Hoosier Classic right after Florida's football team had been put on probation. There was Bobby's wife—the same gal we had felt so sorry for in Las Vegas—sitting up there screaming at Vernon Maxwell and cursing like a sailor. Shortly after that the Knights were divorced.

I was on a clinic with Bobby in Louisville at a time when women's athletics and Title IX was just starting to gain momentum. Several women coaches were sitting in the audience. Before that time, you just didn't see any women at coaching clinics.

Bobby couldn't deal with that. He started off, first of all, by jumping on the women and belittling the Title IX movement. He said they wanted the same money without the same pressure that men's programs were under. "I

think if you're going to get the same money that we do," he told them from the podium, "you ought to get your ass fired just like the men do."

He told three of the foulest jokes I have ever heard in my life, even making a point of doing it because of the women in the audience. He told them that if they were going to come with the men, they'd have to be treated like the men. I think what he did was unbecoming and unnecessary.

Bobby and I got into a tiff that was completely my fault. At the 1987 trials at the Olympic Training Center in Colorado Springs for our various national teams, Vernon Maxwell did not make the first cut-down for either the Pan-Am Games or the World University Games. When asked about it by a reporter, I noted that two of Bobby Knight's players—one a nondescript junior college player—were invited to the World University tryouts that his bosom pal Mike Krzyzewski was holding at Duke. I also said that there are more ways to cheat than giving a kid illegal aid. You can also cheat by promising a kid a tryout or promising a kid a place on one of these national teams if he signs with a certain coach.

Little did I know the reason Vernon didn't make the team was that he had flunked a drug test. When I made my statement, Bobby angrily called Bill Arnsparger, told him about Maxwell's drug test, and threatened to go public with it, breaking the confidentiality that is supposed to exist around Olympic drug tests.

I called Bobby, and he wasn't in. He called back. It was summertime, and we had a young part-time worker named Amy Tyner in the office. Amy took the call and told him I was at our beach condo in Daytona Beach. He asked for the number, and she said she couldn't give it out. She offered to call me and advise that Bobby was trying to reach me. Typical Bobby, he began showering her with profanity.

After a moment, Amy broke in and said, "You know, Mr. Knight, my mother raised me a lot better than your mother raised you. I can tell by your language."

When we hooked up, I apologized to Bobby for reading into the player selections something that apparently wasn't there. I even followed with a letter of apology, explaining that I didn't know about Maxwell's failed drug test.

When I was forced to retire at Florida, Bobby was quoted as saying college basketball was "better off without people like Sloan."

Bobby likes anybody he can beat or browbeat. He doesn't like anyone who will stand up to him and yell back. I think Bobby is an excellent basketball coach, but he is a bully. I don't like those who try to dominate people, but

I would like to think I would never say the game would be better off without Bobby Knight. I don't know that you should say that about anybody in any profession. Everybody with enough ability to stick around for any length of time makes a contribution of some sort.

Though we had a good relationship at first, Bobby and I started falling apart when we beat him in head-to-head recruiting for a big kid named Glenn Sudhop, a seven-foot, two-inch, center out of South Bend, Indiana. When we signed Sudhop at North Carolina State, Bobby started accusing me of all kinds of recruiting irregularities.

The truth was that Sudhop didn't go with Bobby Knight because he didn't think he could take Bobby's kind of pressure. As it turned out, he couldn't take it from me, either. Glenn and I didn't have the best of relationships at State because he didn't want to work hard. I used to tell him he was going to wind up as the tallest used-car salesman in South Bend. I was wrong. He would up as the tallest milling machine operator at International Harvester.

Bobby has always done a fine job wherever he has been. He was a good selection for the Indiana job. I was one of the people who interviewed for that job the year Bobby did. I always considered Indiana to be one of the best jobs in the country because of the great basketball tradition in the state, the pool of talent, and the school's commitment. Also, football wasn't a threat like it was at Ohio State or Michigan. At Indiana, Bobby Knight was the Bull Gator.

Krzyzewski is Scrabble
for Triple-Word Score

Mike Krzyzewski

Mike Krzyzewski was the captain of one of Bob Knight's early Army basket-ball teams. Krzyzewski later became an assistant coach at Indiana before Coach Knight helped him land the head position at Army, which in turn was a giant step on his way to becoming head coach at Duke. Krkzyzewski and Knight have had a falling out in recent years which was detailed in A March to Madness *by the talented John Feinstein.*

Mike Krzyzewski

Mike Krzyzewski had no idea how he felt at the end of his team's four-game run in the 1996 preseason NIT. The Blue Devils played very well in their two home games against St. Joseph's and Vanderbilt, winning both games easily. They struggled, but survived, in their semifinal in Madison Square Garden against a very good Tulsa team.

That victory put them into the final against Indiana. Like it or not, that was going to mean a difficult, emotional evening for Krzyzewski. His relationship with Bob Knight was a complicated one, dating back to the first time Knight had come to his parents' home to recruit him in 1965. Much of what Krzyzewski had become was because of Knight. He had taught him toughness as a player and a system he believed in as both a player and a coach: hard-nosed, man-to-man defense; a motion offense tailored to allow smart players to make smart decisions, and a no-nonsense approach not only to games but even to practices and meetings. He had gotten him started in the business as a graduate assistant at Indiana and had played a role in getting him both of his head coaching jobs, at Army and at Duke.

They had remained close friends for years, doing clinics together in the off-season, talking often on the phone. Krzyzewski had never forgotten what Knight had done for him, and more importantly for his mother, when his dad had died during his senior year at West Point. In 1986, when Krzyzewski took

Duke to the Final Four for the first time, he had Knight speak to his team prior to the semifinals. Knight walked around Dallas that weekend like a proud father, wearing a Duke button everyplace he went.

When Duke lost the final to Louisville, Knight was on the phone with Krzyzewski every night for a week. "Are you OK?" he kept asking. Krzyzewski was fine. He takes losing hard, but he has never taken it as personally as Knight. Still, he appreciated his old coach's concern. A year later, the student and the mentor met in the Sweet Sixteen. Duke, a decided underdog, played Indiana tough before losing to a team that would go on to the national championship. After the game, Knight's first comment was "It's hard for me to enjoy this very much thinking about Mike."

But the relationship now wasn't what it had once been. The 1992 Final Four in Minneapolis had been the turning point. By then, Krzyzewski had won a national championship and became arguably, a bigger star in coaching than Knight. He won just as consistently—in fact, he had been to one more Final Four at that point-and he did it without any of the baggage that Knight brought to the table. Knight was uptight about the match up and told friends before the game that he believed that Krzyzewski had changed with his success, had somehow become less loyal to him.

Krzyzewski heard all this but ignored it. He was convinced Knight was playing a mind game with him, trying to soften his approach to their semifinal. The game was a war, Indiana jumping way ahead, Duke coming back. Knight hurt his team's 'cause with an ill-timed technical foul in the second half and Duke pulled away and appeared headed for an easy win. Then the Hoosiers rallied, actually getting to within three points, with the ball, in the final minute. But Duke hung on for an 81–78 victory.

The post game handshake was not what you might expect between student and teacher. In fact, it was more along the lines of what coaches call a "blow-by," a handshake so quick that no words are exchanged as one coach blows by the other. Krzyzewski was surprised, but not shocked. He knew how much the game meant to him and he assumed it meant just as much to Knight. He hadn't expected a blow-by, but he was prepared for something less than warm and fuzzy.

What he wasn't prepared for was what happened twenty minutes later. At each Final Four, the NCAA curtains off a walkway between the locker rooms and the interview room so coaches and players can walk unimpeded from one to the other. As the losing team, Indiana went to the interview room first. Krzyzewski was walking into the interview room with Christian Laettner and Bobby Hurley just as Knight was leaving. Knight stopped and shook hands with both Laettner and Hurley and wished them luck in the champi-

onship game. OK, Krzyzewski thought, he's got his emotions under control, now we'll shake hands like men and talk for a moment about the game.

Wrong. This time, Knight didn't even look at Krzyzewski. Instead, he looked past him as if he wasn't even there and walked right by him without so much as a nod. Krzyzewski was devastated. Intellectually, he understood what was going on. Knight was a bad loser; always had been. The list of coaches who have turned from good guys into bad ones for having the audacity to beat Knight-especially in a game he really cared about-is a long one. But even knowing all that, Krzyzewski was blown away by the blow off.

He stumbled through his press conference, barely able to keep his mind on the questions. When he walked back to the locker room, he found Mickie, his wife, and his daughters waiting for him. When Mickie put her arms around him to give him a post game victory hug, she was shocked to find him racked with tears.

"What is it?" she asked, completely baffled. "Knight" was the only answer she got.

While his players dressed and answered questions in the Minnesota Twins locker room, Krzyzewski sat in the back with his coaches, his eyes still glistening. "There are days," he said, "when life's not fair."

His team had just qualified for a third straight national championship game and a shot at back-to-back titles and Krzyzewski was completely undone emotionally by his old coach's behavior.

By the next day, he was fine. A number of former Knight players and coaches, having witnessed the initial blow-by in the arena, came by the Duke hotel that night to make sure Krzyzewski was all right. When he told them about the incident in the hallway, they were unsurprised, but nonetheless disappointed in Knight. To a man, they told Krzyzewski to ignore it. "Coach will get over it," one friend said.

"I don't really care if he gets over it or not," Krzyzewski said. "That was it for me."

Ten months passed before the two men spoke again. When word began to leak to the media about a Knight-Krzyzewski schism, it was Knight who took most of the heat. Knight will never admit a battle is lost, but he is always smart enough to understand when it is time to cut his losses.

Shortly after New Year's 1993, he called Krzyzewski. Krzyzewski wouldn't take the call. He kept calling. Finally, on the afternoon that Duke was to play North Carolina in Cameron, Krzyzewski took his call. They talked for about an hour. Knight never said, "I'm sorry," because he never does. What he did do was "explain" to Krzyzewski why he had behaved the way he had. The story was lengthy and convoluted, full of imagined slights, most of which led

back to Krzyzewski having had the audacity to win the game in Minneapolis.

Krzyzewski listened and didn't argue. What was the point? He knew this was as close to an apology as Knight would ever come, and he appreciated the effort. "I'll always love Coach Knight," he said later. "I will always appreciate everything that he did for me. But I think the time has come for us to go our separate ways in life."

Which is exactly what they did. Krzyzewski made a point of never criticizing Knight publicly. In fact, whenever Knight got into trouble one of the people his media sympathizers ran to looking for pro-Knight quotes was Krzyzewski.

Duke and Indiana had played in November of 1995 in the semifinals of the Great Alaska Shootout. That had been Krzyzewski's first weekend back on the bench since his illness the previous season. Duke had won the game 70–64 and had gone on to win the tournament. Facing Knight again-and beating him again-had been cathartic for Krzyzewski. There had been no blowups or blow-bys. Of course, a preseason tournament played in near privacy in Anchorage is a lot different than a Final Four. There was almost no media, and Knight had been cordial.

This was also a November game, but it was a little different. New York was a long way from Anchorage and both teams were nationally ranked. It still wasn't the Final Four by any stretch, but it was important to both coaches as an early-season test of where their teams were and how good they might become. And it was important because they knew the whole country would be watching.

"This is the kind of game you came to Duke to play," Krzyzewski told his team during their afternoon shoot around in Madison Square Garden on the day after Thanksgiving. "Did you see *USA Today* this morning? Banner headline: Duke-Indiana. Anyone who cares about college basketball will be watching this game tonight. That's good. That's the way we like it. That's where Duke basketball is supposed to be."

Indiana was 4–0 and Duke was 3–0. Neither school had won an NCAA tournament game since 1994, which, for these two coaches, represented a major drought. Each suspected that his team was better this year than it had been and each was eager to find out how much better that evening.

This was the match up that NIT officials had hoped for when they put together their sixteen-team draw in the summer. The preseason NIT was twelve years old and, on a number of occasions, attendance in The Garden on Thanksgiving weekend had been embarrassing, with, announced crowds of under 10,000 that looked a lot more like 5,000. That was not a problem for this final. The attendance was 17,930, just shy of a sellout.

Krzyzewski had decided that he was going to take the high road with Knight before the game. He would play the role of dutiful student and greet his old mentor when he arrived at his bench. Knight likes to come out of the locker room at the last possible moment. Krzyzewski knew that. With about two minutes left on the pregame clock, he walked to the Indiana bench to wait for Knight to arrive. He talked to the assistants, even sat on the bench briefly to make things look as informal and comfortable as possible.

The clock ticked down to zero. Still no Knight. The PA announcer began introducing the lineups. Krzyzewski was squirming. Part of his pregame routine is to kneel in front of his bench and give each starter a pat on the back as he is introduced. Still, he waited. Knight finally emerged, walking with famed horse trainer D. Wayne Lucas, a pal of his who was in New York hanging with Knight and the Hoosiers for the weekend.

Krzyzewski was now standing next to the Indiana bench, almost at attention, waiting for his old coach to show up. Knight saw Krzyzewski, stopped, threw an arm around Lucas, and launched into a story. Then he made a point of shaking hands with a few people. By the time he got to Krzyzewski, the teams had been introduced.

Krzyzewski put out his hand. "Good luck," he said,

"You too," Knight answered, turning away quickly.

If it wasn't a blow-by, it was pretty damn close to it. Krzyzewski walked back to his bench angry, but forced himself to forget about it and focus on the game at hand.

Both teams were tight throughout the first half, shooting the ball poorly. Both coaches were on the officials early and Knight, showing what the game meant to him, drew a technical with 5:11 left in the half. That led to a four-point play for Duke and a 28–22 lead. They were still clinging to a six-point margin at halftime, even though Indiana's Andrae Patterson had been virtually unstoppable, scoring 27 of Indiana's 31 points.

"If we get him under control, we'll win the game," Krzyzewski told his assistants at halftime. "None of their other guys are hurting us."

But they never figured out how to stop Patterson. What's more, in the second half, he did get help, most notably from freshman point guard A. J. Guyton, who consistently beat Duke's defense into the lane and ended up with 16 points, six rebounds, and five assists. Patterson had 39 on one of those nights college players dream about.

No one from Duke came close to matching Patterson or Guyton. All five starters shot less than 50 percent and as a team the Blue Devils shot a miserable 35.6 percent. The second half got uglier and uglier. Indiana opened with a 10–2 run to take the lead. Krzyzewski picked up a technical of his own dur-

ing that stretch, arguing over starting center Greg Newton's fourth foul. "You got the second foul," he kept yelling at referee Joe Mingle, implying that Newton had been fouled first. Mingle ignored the comment and ran down the court. "Joe, you guys missed the first foul," Krzyzewski insisted. "You got the second one. Come on!"

For some reason, Mingle decided that comment was worth a technical. When he made the signal and walked to the scorer's table, Krzyzewski really lost it. "Oh fuck you!" he screamed in complete exasperation, loud enough to be heard at least ten rows up. That line didn't earn Krzyzewski a second technical, no doubt in part because Mingle knew he had been trigger-happy on the first one, but also because officials are loathe to toss a coach (two technicals and you're gone), especially a famous one, in front of 17,930 people and a national television audience.

As it turned out, Mingle would have been doing Krzyzewski a favor if he had sent him to the locker room. The Blue Devils were awful down the stretch. Trailing 50–49 with ten minutes left, they managed to get outscored 35–20 the rest of the way. Krzyzewski was on the officials right to the end, but his tone was more plaintive than angry. He knew his team was being outplayed. He just didn't want to concede until he had to.

"What makes me angry is you were outfought," he said to the players when it was over. "I can live with losing if the other team is just better than we are. But you let yourselves get outfought. That's not acceptable."

He didn't get angry or even raise his voice very much. He was frustrated. The entire evening had been frustrating. Sitting with his assistants after he had said all the right things about Indiana in his press conference, he shook his head. "It could be a long season. That just wasn't very good. But we can't afford to jump this team too much. They can't handle it. We've got to almost baby them right now."

The subject of Knight's pregame behavior came up. Krzyzewski sighed. "I'm almost glad it happened that way," he said. "It lets me put a period on the end of the sentence. The end. You know, it's really kind of sad. He keeps turning his friends away. I'm not the first or the last. I tried to do the right thing. I'm over it now. Five years ago, that would have hurt me. It doesn't hurt anymore."

In fact, the most painful part of the evening had much more to do with what Knight's team had been able to do to Krzyzewski's team than anything Knight had done himself to Krzyzewski.

"We play like this," he said finally, "and it's going to be a very long winter."

Experience is What You Get When You Don't Get What You Want

Chris Foster
London Bradley
Butch Carter

Chris, Chris: Maybe it was just the Heimlich Maneuver

Chris Foster

Chris Foster has been a life-long resident of Bloomington, Indiana and led a rather peaceful lifestyle until the Spring of 1999 when he had a fateful encounter with Coach Bob Knight. Foster is a noted guitar maker who has fashioned instruments for some of the top country artists in America

I build musical instruments for a living and I've met a lot of celebrities. When this whole thing came out, I read in the paper that I'm out for my fifteen minutes of fame and that I'd met my first celebrity and was seeking to exploit it. On web sites, I was accused of putting the marks on myself.

It's a long story. Essentially I was in a restaurant and he was at a table in a little town next to Bloomington, called Ellettsville. I overheard comments Knight was making. When I went up to pay my bill, he came up behind me and, basically, I told him that I was offended by some of the things he'd said. He said, "What things?" I told him I didn't think profanity was called for in a public restaurant and that I was particularly upset by his racist comments. The statement that he made that I thought was racist was, "When I have a black player, and he comes into some money, I tell him to buy his mother a house and hang onto the rest of it because when one of those people comes into some money, the rest of them come out of the woodwork." He said that wasn't racist. We were by this time walking out the door; he was ahead of me and I was behind him. I said, 'I'm sorry. But you obviously don't know a racist comment when you make one."

That's when he exploded. He whirled around and grabbed me by the throat, left marks on my neck. The guy I was eating dinner with knocked his hand off my throat and I went in and tried to call the cops. The restaurant people didn't want to tell me where the phone was, but I finally got them to tell me where it was and called the police. I had to say, "Look, I'm calling the police. Where's the damn phone?" They reluctantly did tell me.

Knight has a huge, huge following of fans, and they are religious—bordering on fanatical about it. In fact if you looked at the web sites, especially *The Star,* and *The View* web sites where you have forums where people can discuss whatever, Knight's fans are referred to as lemmings and Kool-Aid drinkers, making reference to Jim Jones.

If you go against Knight, you get your death threats; you get your nasty letters. I've called like the local ReMax realtor to list a property for sale. He

comes out, looks at it and never calls me back. He knows I'm the guy.

Knight will lay out a rash of words at you that you won't believe and then tell everybody that he didn't say anything profane and that he didn't raise his voice. He's really loud. The only time he's not loud is when he's telling you "I said it in this tone of voice." That's the only time he's quiet. And he's profane enough that I don't even think he's aware of it when he is doing it. As far as he's concerned about our run-in, he was just talking "goddamn it, bitch and everything." Nothing really major. But when I first went in, there was a table behind me that had children at it. And so I had thought about what he was saying not really being appropriate. But about halfway through the meal those people left, then one guy came and was sitting there, and he left. So that left Knight's table and mine and when. . . . He was with his wife and her sister and some other woman—three women and him.

The women went outside. I guess as we were going up to pay the bill, they went on out the door and then he's left remaining to pay his bill behind me. I thought his bill had already been paid so I don't know what he was doing behind me—maybe leaving a tip or something. But the women were outside so it wasn't like I walked up to his table and embarrassed him or that anyone overheard what I said. So it was pretty minor. What I kinda wanted to do was clue him in—when you're in public like that and you're making these diatribes that maybe not everyone else wants to hear it. I was just kinda letting him know that I was offended by it and it was loud enough for me to hear and maybe when he's in public or whatever. . . .

You can get all the police reports. Bear in mind—I'm shaking from adrenaline, just been attacked, the police give me a pen and paper and I'm supposed to write down what just happened. One of the errors I made in trying to whip this thing off so I could go—while waiting for the cops to show up in the parking lot, the manager comes out and is talking to Bob Knight. Bob Knight says, "Look if the cops want to talk to me, tell them I'll be at home." And he gives him a card with his number on it and leaves. All the rest of us are still there in the parking lot. He gets three or four days before he finally gives his statement to the police.

I had taken pictures of my welts at a friend's house. I called the cops, then I read that either the prosecutor, Carl Salzmann, is gonna charge him with assault or charge me with provocation. This goes on for a week to ten days. Here in Indiana, no one that I know of has ever been charged with provocation; it's a vaguely upholdable law—I don't know that they use it because you can't uphold it. If I had been black, since I'm white, people chose to look at it as if I were looking for a fight. It was bizarre. After this, the prosecutor walks way out on a limb by defending Knight and not pressing

charges. You can't do anything about a prosecutor. You can't sue him. He's an elected official, right, and he knew a lot of Indiana people wouldn't vote for him if Bob Knight was charged. I can only imagine it was a political choice. Who's not going to vote for him because he threatened to charge the guitar maker? Nobody.

But you go over and try to press charges—I mean look how many IU presidents, like Tom Ehrlich have been run out of town because of Bob Knight. He reprimanded him when he walked off the team with the Russians, and Bob Knight started shopping his resume around. The next thing you knew Tom Ehrlich left town rather than Bob Knight. I saw an old clip on TV where Knight was giving an interview to business people about how he uses choking people as a means of manipulating their behavior.

There was the thing with J. D. Maxwell. When I first had the cops come to the restaurant, they called in the state cops. J. D. Maxwell is an evidence technician for the state police and he also teaches at Bob Knight's basketball camp. He works for Bob Knight, as well as the state police, evidently. He came and the first thing he did was—I was in one state trooper's car, he went up to the guy I was having dinner with and asked him where he worked and told him he knew his boss—as if trying to intimidate him. Then he comes over to me and tells me "No prosecutor's gonna touch this. What did I do to provoke him? Why didn't I just talk to the management? I don't really want to press charges, do I?" I talked to the other state trooper and said, "Look, that other cop's really intimidating and you know I don't know if I should press charges." That trooper said, "Well somebody needs to, he's been getting away with too much." So I said, "Well, let me check with my dad and stepmother, both of whom work for the University." I checked with them and made sure their jobs could handle something like that. Then I called the next day and went ahead and pressed charges.

I called the Superintendent of State Police, Melvin Carraway and told him, "Look, one of your officers was really good, but the other one was completely out of line." He said that he was not investigating officer on this case and that I would have no further problems with him. A few days later, J. D. Maxwell's doing the lead into Bob Knight's press conference saying, "As sure as there's a God in heaven, I knows Bob Knight is no racist." That earned him eight days of suspension, and he was also charged with funneling information about the case to Knight. I believe, and this is totally a guess on my part but, I tend to think that he was involved with locating a witness that didn't exist. Because the prosecutor waited about ten or eleven days to try and decide what he should do. It was when this witness who was a preacher from a town twenty miles away, who said he was at the table next to Knight, but there was

no one at that table. So I don't know where this guy came from but he said he didn't hear Bob Knight cussing but he said he left a couple of minutes before we did. I don't know how he knows when we left if he wasn't there! How could he? Then the "preacher" supposedly had a massive heart attack and is in the hospital and nobody can go talk to him—but we have his statement here, right? Salzmann, the prosecutor, said it was the defining thing. He does claim that Knight grabbed my shirt. It's really unbelievable. I'm forty years old, and first lived in Bloomington in 1962. We've peacefully coexisted for a reasonably long time. Maybe because I deal with so many celebrities, I did not defer to his "celebrity." I thought, "Hey you're a person, you're standing next to me. As far as I'm concerned, you're a person; you just stepped on your dick. I'm gonna let you know you did it. Maybe you'll learn."

This all happened about a year and a half ago. I did get my share of threats and whatever, and it was a big thing and in all the papers. I pretty much didn't give those any more mind than that they were threats. I don't know—there are a lot of people who refuse to see Bob Knight doing anything wrong. They talk about his honesty and his integrity, and he's against hypocrisy. But these are all things he's guilty of.

Theoretically, he got onto this kid for not respecting elders, you know and saying "What's up, Knight?" Yet, this is the same guy who cussed out a 64-year-old woman and threw a potted plant at her. He said, "Oh I might have knocked that plant over accidentally." They accept that—that's true.

When Knight gets ahead of himself, before he realizes the ramifications of his actions, he's already acted. So he immediately goes into damage control mode.

Look into almost any incident with Knight—watch how he handles it. The first thing he does is he gets his lawyers and he gets out of town. He buys himself time—in almost every instance that's what he does. He gets out of town and lets his lawyers deal with it. When he shot the guy in Wisconsin, he didn't take him to the hospital; he got in his car and went straight to his lawyers; the 'chair incident' he goes to Kansas on a recruiting trip; last May on the day of Brand's "zero tolerance" press conference, he left to go fishing; the weekend he got fired, same thing.

John Mellencamp lives here; he's a celebrity. When was the last time you read anything about him encountering people in Bloomington and making national news? Never. You never heard it. It never happens. Joshua Bell lives here, there's I don't know how many accomplished world-class musicians associated with the University and scientists that are celebrities in Bloomington. None of them have this problem. How many coaches are there? If it smells like a rat, it's probably a rat.

Is there a conspiracy against Bob Knight? Either the world's biggest conspiracy or there's got to be some truth to it.

If you look at the kind of guy Knight is. . . . His generation of people— they don't go to a shrink. That does not happen. They don't apologize to you whether or not you just took a beating you didn't deserve or not. There are certain things that I just would describe as "old school mentality." Bob Knight seems to be pretty much the type who subscribes to that. I'm not sure that there aren't a bunch of people who affiliate with those values in some way or see him as some sort of father figure or something to where they're defending something that—most of these people have never been in the same room with him.

Athletic Director, Clarence Doninger said "Tough luck, Coach." After the Ohio State game last year. That's when Knight went off on him. They theoretically have not spoken since. The kid he grabbed, that got him fired, all he said was, "What's up, Knight?" That's all he said. It's really strange.

This spring I watched IU totally defend him. Back when he assaulted me, IU said "This didn't happen on University property and we are gonna stay out of it because it wasn't a university matter." Then when he gave his press conference, he did it out of Assembly Hall, draped with all of IU's prestige. Oddly enough, this was the first one since this press conference from the thing in Puerto Rico.

It's very frustrating. The only avenue left me is to civilly sue Bob Knight. Well, I can't get my lawyer fees back from that because Bob Knight didn't threaten to charge me with a crime. All I can get is my hospital bills and it's just not worth going up against him. I offered to his lawyer, "Look, if he pays my hospital bill, I'll drop charges." But he wouldn't do that.

Our final resolution was the prosecutor couldn't determine one thing or the other. He used the mystery witness to say that he had decided that my story didn't hold enough to be prosecuting Knight and he wasn't going to prosecute me for provocation. He just dropped everything. I thought it was an obvious kangaroo court. Take a look at it. Then it turns out that the state cop was feeding all this information. Bob Knight, at the press conference, said, "If Salzmann was in charge of the Manson case, it would still be undecided and that he'd like to call the whole thing a Mickey Mouse affair except that would insult Mickey Mouse." Knight came out and proceeded to just ream the guy who had just bent over backward doing him a big favor.

You just find yourself vilified on all sorts of different levels. It becomes popular opinion. I've got a friend whose mother read the press accounts and my friend couldn't convince her, having known me for fifteen years, that I didn't do anything wrong . . . but she wouldn't believe her own son. He hasn't

talked to his mom since.—which is the biggest personal thing that I've seen happen as a result of it. She bought the media account.

"Chris Foster is no stranger to law enforcement." Then proceeded to list stuff, the most current of which was fifteen years old. That's hardly means I'm well acquainted with law enforcement. An AP photographer said, "If you piss Knight off, it's forever."

Like the last night when he did his speech to the students in Dunn Meadow after he was fired, he went off the list and litany of all the great players he's had over the years—never mentioned Steve Alford. It's real obvious. I get quite a few calls. When it first happened to me, I had two full notebook pages of media that called but I wasn't talking to them. I gave a brief interview to AP just to get my side of things out and then dodged the rest of it.

London was one of the best referees in the country— the country was Mongolia.

London Bradley

An official that Bob Knight had many run-ins with was London Bradley, now a high-ranking executive with Allstate Insurance in suburban Chicago. London was one of the first black officials in the Big Ten and paved the way for many other minority referees in this country. Bradley was the referee in the 1985 Purdue game who gave Knight the technical foul that caused him to launch the infamous chair across the court. Also, later on in a crucial game against the University of Michigan, Bradley had called a technical on Knight and later, in the eyes of many, Bradley blew a goal-tending call that went against Indiana. Knight came unglued. He was quoted in a national publication as saying, "I did everything but call the guy a "nigger." People are human. If I were a referee, I would tell a guy, 'I'm not gonna call a technical, I'm just gonna throw your ass out.' " That quote sent shock waves throughout the refereeing fraternity.

Nevertheless, London Bradley agreed to an interview for this book and was most gracious and favorable in his comments about Bob Knight. Later Mr. Bradley had second thoughts about that interview and requested that none of his quotes be used.

It's Free Speech only when it's politically correct

Clarence "Butch" Carter

For a man just barely into his forties, Butch Carter has done some amazing things in his life. While not as famous as his younger brother Cris Carter of the Minnesota Vikings, Butch was the Ohio High School Player of the Year in Middletown, Jerry Lucas's home town, before matriculating to Indiana University. He played almost every game in his four years at IU and was the co-MVP of the only NIT Tournament that Indiana has ever won. He made the winning shot with just six seconds to go as the Hoosiers beat Purdue 53–52 in Madison Square Garden. After graduating in four years, he was drafted by the Los Angeles Lakers and spent seven years in the NBA, primarily with the Indiana Pacers. In 1984, while averaging 13.4 a game with the Pacers, he set the all-time NBA record—still standing—for most points scored during overtime in an NBA game. Until recently, he had spent the last ten years as an assistant coach or head coach in the NBA. He led the Toronto Raptors to their first playoff berth ever and he is the winningest coach in Toronto Raptors history. He also holds the distinction of being the only person to become Ohio High School Player of the Year and Ohio High School Coach of the Year in basketball. Carter is the author of "Born to Believe" a book he co-authored with his brother Cris that contains universal positive messages appealing to those searching for meaning. One of the twenty chapters in the book pertain to his relationship with Coach Knight and created quite a stir when the book was released in early 2000. Carter now heads up the Carter Group, a Real Estate Investment and Management firm in Toronto and also is recognized as one of the top motivational speakers in the Ontario province.

Clarence "Butch" Carter

I'm from Ohio and basically went to Indiana 'cause it was one of the few places where all the players were graduating. I was the oldest of seven kids and it was extremely important that I came home with a degree, in my Mom's eyes. What was important to me was that Scott May was from Ohio and Scott had been successful there at Indiana University.

The year (1979) I shot the winning shot at the NIT—it was very important to make it

'cause I had just turned the ball over the possession before. I graduated in four years.

Playing for Bob Knight is tough. The guys who go there are tough guys. You are not going to be practicing with a bunch of soft guys—they're tough guys.

I went back to only one Indiana game, since I left. It was years ago. Knight asked me about being a graduate assistant. I told him things hadn't changed between him and me. He told me he had changed. I told him that he might have changed, but I hadn't changed.

He's a better politician than he is a coach and finally the politicians have turned against him.

Knight got to the point where the people that saved him all these years, the University; he's turned to lying on them. I told one man at the University, "The biggest problem I have on Bob Knight is that you guys have allowed him to use the University as a platform for his lying."

There is the ugly side of him—things that have been hidden because he would threaten to ruin people's lives if you ever exposed anything. People want to be close to someone powerful like that, but he would get on the phone behind people's back and kill people

He threatens guys that challenge him that they won't be able to work or have a meaningful life and he gets away with it.

A painful lesson to learn at any age is how to make friends and also knowing just how and why friendships and acquaintances unravel. It's crucial to make a distinction between sincere friends and acquaintances seeking to exploit the relationship for what you can bring to their lives. A true friendship is built on shared experiences to mutual benefit. A friend loves you for who you are, warts and all, through good experiences and bad, whereas a casual companion or acquaintance seems to like certain parts of you. Developing and maintaining friendships presents certain challenges when you've got a grueling travel schedule.

To complicate relationships, when push comes to shove, you have to put people where they actually are in your life. People whom you thought were friends, you understand later had befriended you, as they wanted something from you, not necessarily because they wanted to contribute positively to your life.

Many cannot and do not understand that this is a method of control and maintaining an illusion of superiority. I think these people are cowards, who will do damage to others by their destructive words and underhanded actions. But people forgive their bullying behavior because they have power.

Knight is an example of this type of person.

When I was an 18 year old freshman at Indiana, Knight gave me a copy of the wonderful Rudyard Kipling poem *If*, which illustrates the positive and negatives of the journey through life. It speaks of hypocrisy and duplicity in a friendship. It's ironic Knight handed it to me, as we are now estranged.

However, the poem remains a poignant source of strength for me. While Knight motivates in a detrimental manner and people do learn from negative lessons, I realized later that he was like many dictators—selfish and ruthless and you just can't get too close to challenging or questioning them. They always have some overt or insidious way of maintaining control and use threats to hold you back. This is different from being a mentor, as a mentor wants the best for you, but doesn't use intimidation and threats as methods to help you develop.

Although with media reports and the actions I witnessed, I don't know if Knight is a racist, but I know he does not like educated strong-willed blacks. He is the kind of man who implies a man should not stand up and be a man; should not have an intelligent opinion. I feel it would be fair to say that he does not like the fact that Cris and I are professionally successful.

This all started when "God" stopped practice early one day. I first heard my mother call Knight "God" during my recruitment. During recruitment, Knight promised he'd be fair to my teammates and me and we would not be subject to segregated behavior. When we were recruited, we thought we'd left these segregated situations behind. One bad day, Knight first threw me out of practice, then threw everyone out, but Knight called me back onto the court while the guys were heading to the locker room. He ripped me up and down. He was still in a rage in the locker room 15 minutes later, going up and down the line. Knight yelled at one of the players (Editor's note: Carter is talking about Isiah Thomas. During Knight's recruiting of Isiah, one of Isiah's brothers "got into it" with Coach Knight at Thomas' Chicago home.) that he would end up like "all the rest of the niggers in Chicago, including your brothers!" An assistant coach, grabbed Knight and pulled him from the room, while Knight screamed that "I don't have to f***** apologize!" I'll never forget looking at that assistant coach, who I greatly admired as a person, yet with Knight's outburst, he couldn't say anything.

When you tell a kid he's going to be like every "nigger" in Chicago, how far is that over the line of inappropriate and cowardly behavior? Knight felt he was at such a superior level that he could make a statement like that to a player in front of his teammates and he had no obligation to apologize to him or the rest of the black players. In effect, not only was Knight talking to that

player, but he was also talking to his two captains. Both of us came from families with many children.

His words and anger affected me, because he was overtly talking about all of us; the eight black players in that locker room and essentially all the black players he had ever coached. All these players had put money in his pockets and helped win Big Ten and National Championships, yet he was hypocritical and deliberately chose to say what he truly felt about us.

We all got dressed quickly and scattered, knowing that his tirade could have been directed at any one of us. I felt sorry for that individual player, but he said not to worry about it as he had decided to leave the next year. The talented player could have chosen any college, with a scholarship, but he had chosen to go to Indiana. Knight had shown his deepest, darkest thoughts and resentment to him and everyone in the locker room had witnessed the display.

Knight never did apologize—that day, nor in the week or months afterward. It was as if it had never even dawned on him that his behavior and that incident might not only be unacceptable, but hurtful in the long run.

Even after the years have passed and I was doing everything possible to move away from that incident, it haunted me. A former Indiana teammate who was also in the locker room that day, sat down with me at a restaurant a couple of years back. Randy Wittman is now head coach of Cleveland Cavaliers and he was upset with me, saying he heard I'd been saying Knight is racist. I had never talked about the incidents at Indiana I'm describing—I've never mentioned them to family members, friends, nor discussed it with those teammates.

I asked Randy, 'You sat there in the locker room and heard the same thing I did. What part of it did you not understand?' Even if he didn't think the comment was racist, was Knight just having a bad day? How did I end up getting the blame for what Knight said? I left there thinking that here's this guy coaching in the NBA and how is he ever going to be fair to his black players if he takes that stand on that statement? He did it because of intimidation and widespread acceptance of Knight's behavior. This reminded me again of the poem's validity and especially the first two lines.

Another incident that happened after a practice in my first season was the final straw in having any trust in Knight. That year he had also denounced a former player in the locker room in front of our team, who was in his rookie year with the Milwaukee Bucks. (Editor's note: The only Bucks' rookie from Indiana that year was Quinn Buckner.) The team was visiting Indiana for a game with the Indiana Pacers and the player had taken the time to drive down to talk to Knight. He was evidently having personal problems and

thought he was discussing them in private. Knight immediately came down from this meeting and talked to the team and told us the intimate details. With no thought of discretion or sensitivity, Knight shamelessly used their discussion as an example of why we needed to listen to him in making decisions to avoid making mistakes.

That's what turned me totally away from Knight—doing what he did to that man was cowardly. And it was totally unnecessary. It was self-serving— it was none of our business what was going on in this player's life and I was even more disgusted since this player had helped to recruit me to Indiana. I left the locker room in a furious state. This man had trusted Knight with the most intimate details of his personal life and Knight used it to make himself look good.

Half the guys in the locker room didn't even know the player personally and after the incident of Knight's locker room explosion at the black player combined with this, I knew I was never to trust this man with anything going on in my life. Not only was Knight clearly not a friend, he was a self-serving coward who masqueraded as a confidant.

If Knight was angry, he usually was angry at me first as I was the the team captain. With two starters out with injuries, it showed in our early record. Knight knew I was the first in conditioning, but told me I was to be the sixth man, and was not even allowed to compete for a starting spot that season. We were in a position to win the Big Ten Championship, on the strength of Isiah Thomas. Luckily, his sheer talent was so impressive that Knight overlooked situations, and it was a constant pleasure to me that he would have to bend to the will of Isiah. And, Isiah did not let Knight stop him from developing his natural talent.

Still, he'd take me out of the game if anyone else made a mistake. After one particular game where he benched me and let us lose the game, I called a friend who worked at the university. He said that if I was going to listen to everything Knight said, I wasn't going to be able to play. He was right, and I'll bet he gave that speech many times. I just decided not to listen to Knight and I overcame whatever he put in my way.

Most players were forced to play a level of basketball they might not have reached otherwise, and a lot of good players have come out of Indiana. There are no gray areas there—you're either a successful player or you're not.

How did these players—these men—swallow their pride to accomplish a more important goal of teamwork, winning and taking instruction? We buried any feelings of personal boldness and became a versatile, strong and powerful team. Some people do well in a prescriptive, militaristic environ-

ment where they adapt well to being told what to do. Some don't and bury their personal feelings, which is destructive. In this case, winning wasn't everything.

Knight always used to say, "I've forgotten more about basketball than you'll know." That's especially true since he's a better politician than he is a coach. For example, he said his practices were closed, but then we'd see his favorite trustee of the moment or the president of the university at practice, so we knew it would be easy practice and we'd get the hard practice later.

He always told us that when you win games, people continue to accept whatever you do and he has proved that over and over again. Swearing was a common way for him to express his anger but that was tolerated as well as his explosive physical actions such as throwing or kicking objects. I understood him so well because he was so predictable; one of the most predictable people who have been part of my life. He understands most people are weak and shy away from confrontation.

When incidents like these happen in life to you, or if you are an observer, you think by being quiet or with time it will go away. But it doesn't go away. Continuously throughout my process to become a head coach, in college and in the pros, people fed off the fact that I did not have a strong relationship with Knight.

One athletic director (editor's note: The University of Toledo) told me in an interview for his head coach's job that he thought he needed Knight's recommendation. I was up for a college job and it was one of the few times I've lost my temper. I specifically told him that if he needed Knight's recommendation, I didn't want the job. The guy talked to Knight and I didn't get the job because Knight discouraged him from hiring me. I played for Knight, was his captain, and I graduated on time, yet he had the power to defeat me professionally. But the way the system is set up in the United States, you can pick up the phone and assassinate someone's character, as it's the politics of the game. Interviewers don't check because it's the perception that counts.

For some reason, Knight can't acknowledge he's one of those old-style, intimidating personalities who's got seasoned athletes and coaching peers quaking in their sneakers rather than talk about him publicly. It's understandable as many bide their time and are worried about the repercussions of confrontation. The fact is, when you deny stories, you actually then are accepting and perpetuating cowardly behavior. It's a detriment to the public, the league, players, and the families of athletes being recruited. Dark private thoughts are just that, and the ones who are hurting are the people who don't acknowledge his harmful private behavior.

I don't for a moment expect others to acknowledge these particular incidents as we've all got a lot on the line, but I wouldn't be true to myself it I kept it hidden. Some people say "forgive and forget," but if we all did that, we'd forget crimes and the large acts of irresponsibility and abuse. Besides, it reinforces the best way I've learned how to deal with controversy and static; deal with it head on and move on.

I mentioned earlier that I don't believe you rise up by stepping on people; your job in life is to help people rise up as you rise. Unfortunately, there are people who stomp on you as you rise. Don't accept it. You may have to wait a few years before you understand what was happening and how to make it right for you, but don't hold on to destructive relationships or thoughts.

And, of course, beware of cowards.

The bad part about my book was that my timing was bad. I didn't know that shit with Neil Reed was coming out so everybody thought I was just piling onto what Reed was doing. That wasn't the case. We started our project the prior summer and it would have been out last Christmas, but my brother, Cris, didn't get his part written.

As far as I know Quinn Buckner never knew that Knight came down to the locker room and talked about the intimate details of their conversation. Quinn has seen my book, but he doesn't know that he is the former player I was referring to.

I had written a book involving Knight once before. It happened way back in 1988, I submitted it to a writer, Mark Katz, of the Dayton Daily News, and he begged me not to do it. He said, "Butch, don't do it—don't do it." The whole thing is everybody wants to believe there's very few cases where someone actually kisses a lot of asses and gets ahead. Mark was thinking "You're gonna hurt yourself—you're gonna hurt yourself." I held it for that long. But that's the way it works out.

That week the book came out, Marcus Camby called to say I was a liar. It wasn't the fact that he might know anything about Isiah, Knight and me. It was the fact that I had traded Marcus to New York.

I said, "To hell with this guy calling me a liar." I filed a slander suit because Marcus has already been convicted of lying to a grand jury on the UMass thing. And, obviously he had no clue about this situation as he was a toddler when it happened.

Marcus Camby's manager was the Public Relations Director for the Toronto Raptors when we drafted him and was hired by Isiah. Isiah left the Raptors and that guy left with Isiah, to manage Isiah. Then when we traded Marcus to New York, he started managing Marcus. So Isiah and him put

Marcus up to attacking me because Isiah was 'in bed' with Bobby Knight in order to get the Indiana Pacers' job. Isiah was the one who came out and defended Bobby Knight last spring because Isiah was so desperate to get back into pro basketball. The only opportunity that was available to him was Indiana and if he comes out and admits that Knight has said that to him, there's no way the Pacers can hire him. I know all that; Isiah hated Knight. But Isiah sold his soul to get the Indiana Pacer job. He sold it to Knight.

Isiah put Marcus Camby up to calling me a liar. The thing is I had to send the message up to Isiah and the next one who called me a liar I was going to sue them. The last thing Knight and them wanted was to be in court and everybody would have to stand up under oath and tell the truth about what happened.

That's what I told the NBA committee when I talked to them when they were reviewing my Knight statements. I said, "I got no problem with what Knight said. If you read my book, you'll understand that to me it wasn't the matter of that. The problem I have is that Knight is a coward—anything that goes wrong in Indiana if you don't buy into what he says, even if you go away and keep your mouth shut, he tries to destroy you. He lies and gets other people to lie to destroy people's lives. If this hadn't come out on Neil Reed, you guys would be sitting there saying it never happened and you would have hundreds of people lie to you.

This was after the whole state felt good about Larry Bird, who was one of the few people who overcame Bobby Knight. He really has. Knight, basically, didn't give a fuck that Bird left school because Knight's attitude is "If you don't go to Indiana, your life's all fucked up." Bird went to Indiana State, then goes to play for the Celtics. Bird had left the year or two before I got to Indiana.

I just knew that people in the coaching fraternity like to think of certain schools as 'family,' and that I wasn't in the kiss-ass Indiana family. That didn't bother me at all. It's just the way it works.

The Last Chapter

The last chapter of *Knightmares* is yet to be written.

It would have been written Sunday but the author watched football.